# These Truths

## Joe Zeppetello

# PRAISE FOR *THESE TRUTHS*

In *These Truths*, Joe Zeppetello provides a sardonic take on this day and age of 24-hour news cycles and endless spin, skillfully weaving a tale of the hue and outcry that might result from a startling revelation about one of the Founding Fathers – a perfect storm that very nearly ruins the lives of the researchers who uncover the truth.

> ~Howard Massey, author of *Roadie, The Great British Recording Studios*, and co-author of Beatles engineer Geoff Emerick's memoir *Here, There and Everywhere*.

If you're going to write a novel about people grappling with hard truths, you'd best have Joe Zeppetello's humility. He never gets in the way of this gripping, driven tale of the many faces of piracy. Here are people, unlike millions of Americans, hell-bent on truth, and their stories sound as if they voted for Joe Zeppetello to tell them.

> ~Djelloul Marbrook, critically acclaimed poet and prose writer, and author of several collections of poetry, novels, and novellas, including *The Seas are Dolphins' Tears*.

This book is dedicated to the memory
of my brother Tony—one of my biggest fans.

# Acknowledgments

To my wife, Lyza, who read at least one version of this book, and to Vicki Sarkisian, who also read more than one version.

And to the members of Glaring Omissions, my writing group, whose contributions and suggestions were always helpful: Scott Anderson, Suzanne Bennet, Miriam Ben-Yaacov, Elle Cage, Will Nixon, Guy Reed, and Violet Snow.

# Preamble

*Early 1700s*

Jean had never seen water as blue as he gazed from the deck of the ship entering Kingston Harbor, Jamaica. While he was in Louisiana, he had worked in the salt works, boiling seawater down to make salt, but it was usually more brown than blue. Like all the slaves on Cannel Island, Jean worked hard; some tended the sugar cane fields, while others boiled down salt and shoveled it into barrels. Sometimes Jean could catch a glimpse of the bay, but if he looked too long, a driver would threaten him with the whip. That didn't stop him from gazing out to sea whenever he had the chance. Somehow, he knew that was his best chance to escape.

His thoughts drifted to his mother. She'd been a housekeeper slave, kidnapped from Senegal before she was old enough to marry, but not before she'd been educated in a French missionary school. Her master had been more generous than most, and had allowed her to keep her son near her. She had taught him to read and write. But a crash in sugar prices caused by new large sugar cane plantations in the Caribbean had bankrupted him. She was sold to a plantation near New Orleans as a house maid, and Jean to the Cannel Island Planation. He remembered her being put on the back of an open wagon, her hands in chains, her deep brown eyes open wide with hate and indignation. She leaned over to him and whispered in his ear before the drivers with their whips could pull them apart, "Don't let them know you can read and write, Jean. That's how you will get free. Don't let them know. Someday you will get a chance. When that comes, you leave. Don't look for me, just go as a far away as you can."

***

Jean was reading a newspaper that the master had thrown out. The shipping and commerce news listed all the ships coming into the port of New Orleans. Their island was about twenty-five miles southeast of the port. Most ships leaving New Orleans for the Gulf of Mexico and points south would have to go by them just a few miles out in the main channel. A weekly newspaper published the times when ships were expected to arrive, to leave, where they were coming from, and where they were bound.

A plan was forming in the back of his mind.

He heard a noise behind him, and quickly turned the paper upside down, scrutinizing it with his brow furrowed as if in concentration.

"What you doin' there, Ju-an?" Frederick, one of the white drivers, pronounced his name as if it was Spanish, and put in two syllables. First he looked at Jean, and then at the paper. Frederick was confused for a minute, and then barked a loud laugh. Jean looked at him and rolled his eyes. looking down at the ground.

"I jus' found this on the ground, sir. Is it yours?" He handed the paper to Frederick, who tore it out of his hand.

"No, it ain't mine, stupid. And don't be pretendin' you can read. You's holdin' the dang thing upside down."

***

A few weeks later, while looking out over the bay, he noticed what he thought might be a half-submerged box that had hung up on a clump of seaweed. As he looked closer, he felt a surge of recognition. It wasn't a box at all, but rather a submerged boat, a small skiff that must have broken loose upstream during a storm. He quickly hauled it in and had just finished covering it when one of the drivers, a young black man named Marcus, who stood a good foot taller than the next tallest man on the island, found him. While most of the drivers were white, a few were blacks who had privileges. Some were even paid and were saving up to buy their freedom. Marcus was fair-minded, but he didn't shy away from punishment. In fact, he was more prone to punish an unruly slave than most of the white drivers; otherwise they might call him soft.

Jean pulled up on his pants. "Nature called, and I had to go." Marcus looked at him, fingering his whip, his truncheon tucked in his belt. He motioned with his head to get back to the salt works, whacking Jean hard across the back of the legs with the truncheon for good measure as he walked past.

"I ain't stupid," Marcus said plain and simple with no inflection in his voice.

Jean didn't feel the pain. His mind was whirling with plans on how to escape. He didn't notice that Marcus looked directly at the pile of seaweed and driftwood covering his boat.

Since they were on an island, the slaves weren't locked down at night. There was no place they could run to, so no need to bother. Jean carefully slipped out of his bed and made his way to the shore. The boat was in better shape than he could have hoped for: it had been swamped, but there was minimal damage except for a gash in the gunwale. He suspected the skiff must have been a lifeboat that had broken loose in a storm and probably smashed into the side of the ship as it fell. He could fix it with a few small boards, a couple of nails, and some tar, but he'd need some oars. Jean worked on the boat until the east started to get lighter, and then snuck back to his bed. He did so every night for two weeks. Fixing the gash in the side of the gunwale was easy enough, but it took some doing to get all the parts to make two respectable oars. A couple of old broom handles and scrap wood worked out well. He kept an eye out for discarded newspapers in order to finish his plan. He found one in the trash, quickly read the shipping and commerce news, and finally saw what he was looking for. He smiled as he checked the shoreline for the tide and calculated in his head the time he'd need to leave. He shoveled salt all afternoon; it was well into twilight when work was finally stopped. After his supper, he went to the slave's quarters and pretended to sleep.

Quietly, Jean slipped out of the quarters and went to the shore. He untied his boat and pulled off the mound of seaweed covering it, checked the oars and supplies, and tried to push it out into the bay, but a strong wind had come up, and the surf kept pushing him back. He gave a mighty heave and grabbed onto the back of the skiff, but the waves shoved him back to the shore smashing him between the boat and the rocks, cracking his ribs. Jean tried again, pushing for all he was worth, his side screaming at him in pain. The sea took him out, then sent him careening back to shore, and then sucked him and the boat back out to deep water. Jean hit his head against the rocks. Everything was getting black, and he slipped under the water, letting go of the boat. He'd never been in water over his head and had no idea how to a swim. As he tried to claw up to the surface, the waves pushed the boat back on top of him and he slammed into the bottom of it. His lungs fought for air, trying to force him to take a breath. He fought to keep from breathing in the water that would kill him. Just as he blacked out, he felt a hand grab him and pull him up. Then he felt himself pulled into the boat. He opened his eyes and saw Marcus's face framed in the bright moonlight.

"For bein' so smart, you shore is stupid. Don't you even knows how to swim?" Marcus sat down in the center seat facing the back of the boat and started pulling on the oars, slowly moving the small boat away from land. "Used to work as a fisherman," he said, studying the tips of the oars. "You done a good job on these oars, but this boat has seen better days. Bottom is all ate up by shipworm."

Jean was still out of breath but recovered enough to say. "Marcus?"

"Yeah? You still think I'm dumb, right?" he said. Jean shook his head. "Now don't you lie none. Everyone think Marcus is stupid because that's how Marcus wants them to think. I seen you readin' them papers. I watched you fix this here boat. How do you think you found all the stuff you needed? I left it for you to find! You got a plan, and Marcus wants in."

"Yeah. I got a plan," Jean was getting his voice back. He moved from the bottom of the boat to the seat in the front, while Marcus pulled on the oars. Jean held his aching side and looked at the stars, blinking away the double vision caused by the blow to his head, quickly finding the Big Dipper and then facing the North Star. He pointed to his right. "We gotta go that way, to the east. We gotta get into the main channel, where the water is deep and there aren't any shoals."

They rowed until daybreak, each taking turns with the oars, Jean constantly looking at the horizon. Finally, he saw a ship; he hoped it was the one he was looking for. "Make for that ship," he told Marcus.

"Won't they just make slaves of us, too? Or take us back?"

"Not if they're Quakers. My mom told me about them. They white, but they don't believe in slavery. That ship should be the *Welcome* sailing out of Philadelphia, bound for Jamaica."

"I hope you right."

"Me, too."

***

The sailor in the crow's nest of the *Welcome* looked four times through his telescope before alerting the first mate, shaking his head all the while. Two black men in a tiny sinking skiff were waving frantically at the ship. The first mate shouted an order and spilled wind from the sails to slow them down. The captain, hastily dressed in his long black coat and large-brimmed hat, was on deck as soon as he felt the change in speed, although he had been in a deep sleep. The first mate filled him in, and they launched a twenty-foot dory to rescue the men. As the dory got closer, it was clear that the small skiff was now underwater, and the men were hanging onto the sides. In about an hour, they were on board and brought to the captain.

"We are slaves who have escaped from Cannel Island," Jean said in halting English. "Since you are Quakers, I thought you could take us to Jamaica and to freedom."

The captain thought for a moment, and then burst out laughing.

"Well, you are brave men indeed, but there is at least as much slavery in Jamaica as there is in Louisiana. I will take you there, and as I am from Germantown and a follower of William Edmundson, I will treat you as the freemen that God made you, but beware, there are many even of my faith, fellow Friends, who would not. Since you are free men, you must pay for your passage. After you rest and eat, I expect you to work for your fare. I'm sure my first mate can find adequate work for you." With that, the captain went back below deck to finish his interrupted sleep.

*Six Years Later*

A cannonball flew across the bow of the colonial merchant ship flying an English flag. A Corsair flying the flag of France, a privateer, had been gaining on them for the past few hours. There was no hope for an English Man-O-War coming to the rescue. The captain of the merchant ship, though, held his course. The next cannonball took out the mizzenmast, and the ship slowed. There were no soldiers aboard the merchant ship, and no cannon, so the captain struck his sails and literally stopped the ship, waiting for the pirates to catch up. Their only hope was mercy, and that was in short supply in Caribbean pirates. They were astonished that the man in charge of the pirate ship, and most of the crew were black. The name of the ship painted on the side was the *Rogue Noir*. A wiry black man with a sword at his side and a pistol tucked in his belt came aboard the ship. He spoke English accented with French.

"I am Jean, captain of the *Rogue Noir*. Some have called me Jean the Mulatto, or Black Caesar. You are in no danger as long as you don't resist. We are only interested in your cargo." Jean looked at the merchant captain and noticed his long black coat and broad-brimmed hat. "Where do you hail from?" he asked.

"We are from Philadelphia."

"Are you Quakers?"

"Yes, we are of the Society of Friends."

"What do you say, Marcus?" Jean called back to his ship. Marcus came forward, stooping so as not to knock his head on the boom. The sword at his side was longer than some men, and he carried a brace of pistols in his belt.

"They are Quakers?"

"Yes."

"Then we leave them be as written in our laws."

"There will be no plunder today, men," Jean shouted to his crew. "It is in our Charter that we do not capture Quaker ships."

"You have a Charter?" the captain of the merchant ship asked in disbelief.

"Of course," Jean replied, as if to a child. "How else would we be able to work together? We have rules, and every man on board has sworn allegiance to the Charter. Marcus and I were saved by a Quaker ship, so we return the favor to all Friends." He paused to look at the broken mizzenmast. "Your main mast is still intact; you can make it back to port for repairs or continue on. No reason you can't still make it to the Canary

Islands to have the mast repaired there before you continue on your journey," he said as he left. He ordered the grappling hooks retrieved, and the men shoved the two ships apart. Jean and Marcus stood on the bridge as the *Rogue* turned away from the merchant ship. Confused and still a little dazed, the captain ordered the sails to be hoisted on his ship's remaining masts and turned east, catching the trade winds, looking over his shoulder, not quite believing what just happened.

"The men are angry about that," Marcus said. "That ship was loaded with expensive trade goods and plenty of rum; we could have gotten decent money for them at Port-au-Prince."

"Maybe it's time to read them the Charter again?"

"Maybe," Marcus said as he crossed the deck and went below. A few minutes later, he emerged with a document written with black India ink on vellum, rolled up and tied with a piece of green silk cloth. It had been written by Jean when the ship was first commissioned by the French king, and they'd been given a Letter of Course that entitled them to attack Spanish and English ships in the name of France. Every member of the crew had sworn allegiance to the Charter. Marcus handed it to Jean, and then called the crew to general quarters. They all assembled before the bridge and looked up to their captain. Jean unrolled the Charter and began to read,

"We the people of the *Rogue Noir*, in order to form a more perfect union, hold these truths to be self-evident: that all men are created equal and have the right to life, liberty and brotherhood ...."

# Chapter 1

*21st Century*
*Bradbury College, Hudson Valley, New York*

"You children have no business reading *Moby Dick*. You need to be at least thirty to understand that book, and then only if you've been paying close attention your whole life. And if you haven't been paying any attention at all, like most Americans, then you don't have a hope in hell of understanding *Moby Dick*. How old are all of you? Twenty? Eighteen? For God's sakes, if it were up to me, we'd just forget about the whole thing right now. However, the English Department decided that you should read this book, so we're going to read it, and maybe, just maybe, you'll get a glimmering of what it's all about, those of you who actually read it, and not the rest of you who will just glance at Sparknotes." Professor Gilbert Sykes paused for a moment to look out over the American Romanticism class of over seventy students.

"So how many of you overly coddled, spoiled children have actually bought the book?" A few students carefully raised their hands. "Good, now you guys come down here and sit in the front. The rest of you I would respectfully ask to drop the class immediately to avoid the chore of me having to fail you in December. But you won't. I'm sure you'll stick it out to the bitter end, learning nothing, wasting my time and your parents' money, but that's the way things are. Who am I to complain?"

He waited. A few students had left while he had them change their seats. One young man put his hand up.

"Yes?"

"The bookstore didn't have any copies left," he said.

"Why doesn't that surprise me?" Sykes asked no one in particular. "That's par for the course for them. Maybe you can get a bunch of people together and buy them online? Pay extra for overnight shipping? It'll probably be cheaper than the usurious markup in that store anyway. But don't tell anyone I said that. You understand?" The boy nodded.

"Who of you needs, actually wants, and will maybe even read the book?" Sykes asked the class. A bunch of hands went up. Sykes knew it was amazing what a little fear could do. "Then contact," he pointed to the student who'd told him the book was not in, "what's your name, son?"

"Billiam," the boy said.

Sykes made a face. "You must have deeply confused parents," he said under his breath, and then turned to the whole class, "Everyone who does not have a book, you need to get hold of … Billiam after class, and all of you place an order and split the overnight charges. The book doesn't cost very much; it's one tenth the price of your business management book, but then there's nothing in it you really need to know to help you make any money, so I guess it works out."

He picked up a stack of papers. "Here's your syllabus. As you can see, you're at least two chapters behind already, and this is the first day of class. Expect to be behind the whole semester, and you will not be disappointed. And after you lose this copy, you can go to the class website and get it online."

***

He walked across campus, enjoying the pleasant late summer day. He could see the Hudson through the trees. The crew team was out on the river, rowing parallel to shore. They were pretty well coordinated, so it was probably the varsity crew. It took a long time for a crew to really work together that well. The summer had been hot, so there no real trace of a change of leaf color yet, and students were sunning themselves outside the dorms. He had his freshman class in the new lecture halls, since they were the largest on campus, and was now on his way to a senior seminar. There he would be giving the seniors what he liked to call their "first taste of graduate school." His seminar was always full, and he never turned away any senior who really wanted to take it.

There were some familiar faces, since the school was small, and the department was also pretty small. He handed out the syllabus and talked for a while, asking them questions to see what they actually knew, what sort of literature interested them, what they might have already read, and how much of it they'd already forgotten. They were a strong bunch of students, so it would probably be a good class, but, as he reminded himself, he'd been fooled before. He'd just had a nightmare advanced writing class the previous year where not one of the students seemed to be able to manage to get the weekly page count finished on time for discussion. Often the students would come running into class, late, with pages hot from the laser printer, or upload their work to the course website just before class. These practices used up comment time because people had to sit and read the text first, during class time. No end of threats from him seemed to motivate them to get their work in on time.

Occasionally this happened, and Gil had a theory: Classes needed a balance between alpha and beta students. Alpha students were the first to raise their hands, had all the work done on time, and usually read enough of the assignment to make good comments. Beta students tended to make fewer contributions to class even if they had read everything, but were not prone to comment without prodding, often considered deadlines a suggestion, but would turn in papers on time if others did in order to not look bad. Too many alpha students could make a chaotic class with a lot of superficial discussion, and too many beta students could make a very quiet class. And the personality type had nothing to do with a student's ability. He had seen plenty of alpha students who tended to be superficial and repetitive, and sometimes formulaic in their papers and responses. Good beta students tended to think more deeply, but poor beta students tended to be unmotivated and lazy. Good alpha students kept the class going; good beta students could interject a thoughtful analysis in class discussion at crucial points.

He finished his second class, went for a late lunch to one of the school cafeterias, and then walked back to his office. In the mailroom, the dean's secretary stopped him and said that the dean wanted to see him.

Gilbert Sykes went to the dean's office and sat in one of the chairs facing the desk. Dean Malone was finishing up a phone call with someone she obviously wanted to end long before they actually hung up. She smiled at Gil and frowned at the phone. Finally, she hung up.

"Gil," she said, "what the hell? We just started this week and I'm getting calls about you already. Parents are screaming at me."

"Sorry, Pat. I can't sugarcoat the fact that they're ignorant. It's not their fault, of course, considering the imbeciles who tend to get elected to school boards these days, not to mention the ghastly teachers, and insipid, supercilious administrators, but nonetheless, the kids don't know a thing."

"They were high school seniors three months ago for goodness sake, not Rhodes Scholars."

"Since when do you listen to the parents? What do they have to do with it? My father would never have called my college when I was an undergrad. It would never have occurred to him. I think that he wasn't even quite sure where the college was until I graduated." Gilbert said, his eyes blinking defensively behind his glasses.

"That's not the point. Could you try to teach American Lit without scaring the crap out of them?"

"I could be more touchy feely." He stroked his chin. "Maybe we could read some of *Moby Dick*, certainly not all of it, that would be expecting far too much, and sit in a circle to tell each other how we all felt about it?"

"Gil, please stop," Pat said.

"Sorry," he replied, "You are one of the good guys."

"Thanks."

"I was chair of your search committee," he reminded her. She'd been hired as a specialist in Modernism but had found that she had a talent for administration. She also had a work-averse husband who was a writer but had yet to finish a novel after fifteen years of trying, or get a job, or help very much with their three kids who were closing in on college age, so she had become the dean a few years back.

"Yes. You were. I almost passed up the job because of you."

"Nonsense."

"Nope, it's true. I'd never lie to you, Gil." She smiled, but then got serious. "Look, Gil, some of this drivel is percolating up the ladder. One of the kids you frightened this week is the nephew of a big donor."

"You mean he put some money into the football team?"

"Actually, he donated an academic building."

"Really? I didn't know our donors even knew that we had academic buildings."

"We haven't heard anything from him, just the kid's parents."

"Okay. You want me to bring him a bagel and a cup of coffee next class?"

"Gil!" Pat sighed and looked out the window across campus. Classes were changing, and the sidewalks were crowded with students. She always found that sight reassuring. "When was your last sabbatical?"

"I'm about due. Might not come back if I leave, though. Retirement sounds fine right now."

"You wouldn't dare." She grinned, and then pleaded with him, "Just tone it down a bit, please?"

"For you, Pat, anything." Gil winked. "Anything else?"

"No, not really, just be sure your department gets the self-study done. It was supposed to be in at the end of July." Her phone rang.

"Really? I was wondering if we should include a selfie on the cover with the whole department. Maybe we could take it in front of the new football stadium?"

"Bye, Gil," Pat said as she answered the phone while waving him out the door.

Gil nodded a greeting to the secretary who had a line of students at her desk, and walked the length of the hallway to his office at the far end of the building. He had chosen the office that was physically the farthest from the main office in hopes that students would simply give up or get lost on their way. The strategy hadn't worked out well. He closed the door quickly and left the overhead light off so the window over his door would remain dark, as if no one was inside. His office hours didn't start for a while, and he had to catch up with some work. The desktop was on, but required some updating, so he waited while it was security checked by the school mainframe before it allowed him access to his email or the internet.

There had been a huge scandal ten years back, with a team of students and a few teachers making pornos in the media lab and then selling them online. Apparently the father of one of the students involved recognized his daughter in a video, and then the oatmeal really hit the fan. No one did ever ask the guy exactly what he was doing on a porno site, but that seemed beside the point in the larger scheme of things. The new head computer geek who took over from the old head computer geek who had immediately resigned made a lot of changes in security. Actually, Gil reflected, any changes would have been a lot, since there had been, essentially, no security at all.

The student entrepreneur who had organized the whole thing was allowed to graduate because she blamed it all on the faculty members, who were promptly fired. Of course, they should have known better. She was now the youngest CFO of a Fortune 500 company, and on the Bradbury Board of Trustees, donating a ton of tax-deductible money to the Media Arts Department each year, a grateful gesture for learning the most important lesson in American business: Always have someone else to take the fall for your mistakes.

Gil had barely opened the cup of coffee he'd bought at the cafeteria after he finished his lunch when his email box finally opened on his desktop. There were the usual general "welcome back" emails from the various departments and clubs, which Gil deleted, unopened, and then there was an email from an address he didn't recognize at first: Valerie Dymond, a specialist in American colonial literature who was on the faculty of Chamberlain, a small college on the other side of the Hudson, about half an hour away. They had put several panels together at conferences because they had similar research interests, and Gil had liked her presentations.

He remembered her as being never politically correct, favoring either the liberal or conservative interpretations of colonial literature. Nor was she very postmodern. Her findings were more from the point of view of a cultural anthropologist than a literary critic. They were what he would rationally have expected.

He thought back to the first conversation they'd had after he had heard her presentation on early colonial literature at a national conference. Many people in the audience hadn't liked the simple way she stuck to the facts in her anthropological technique. She didn't embellish or minimize the conditions of the colonies in North America during the two hundred years before the Revolution.

"So most of the writings in the Colonial period were from white men of leisure?" Gil asked as he brought them each a coffee from the large carafe that was in the corner of the meeting room. "I'm astonished."

"I know that some people want to romanticize the power of women and slaves, but the bottom line was that they had none, not in this time period." Valerie sipped her coffee. "Don't get me wrong. We'd all just love to discover another Phillis Wheatly or Anne Bradstreet; they just don't exist. That's why such women are studied so intensely, because they're so rare." Valerie was glad the presentation was over. It always made her nervous to stand in front of her peers and read her latest research. She had not slept well and had skipped breakfast.

"I agree. I've often thought some of our colleagues are a little too eager to find the next great slave narrative or personal journal at the expense of ignoring glaring realities about the time period and the place."

"You mean the fact that, as I pointed out, the mixture of Calvinism and capitalism in Colonial America gave very few the time to write, and most of them who could write were preachers or self-satisfied businessmen, so we have plenty of sermons from guys like Jonathan Edwards and a few personal diaries from businessmen, all full of the thoughtless racism and sexism of the time."

"These were not modern people by any standards. But their message that poor people are poor because they're lazy and God wants them to be poor, whereas rich people are wealthy because God gave them the money is a message that many rich people love to hear today, with no mention of greed or materialism, of course."

"You've got that right." Val raised her coffee cup, and she and Gil touched the two paper cups together in a toast. "Some things never change."

They made it a point from then on to meet at conferences, and they sometimes presented together. Whenever Gil hit a snag with his work, he would contact Valerie, and the same went for her.

Valerie's email asked him to call. Gil checked the time, and figured that she'd probably be in class, so he finished reading his email, then opened his door for office hours, and took a book off the shelf to read for class. It wasn't long before he was joined by a young man in shorts and flip flops in spite of the coolness of the day.

"Professor Sykes?"

"In person," Gil said.

"I need you to sign an override."

"For?"

"Your class."

"I'm teaching three of them this semester; which are you interested in attending?"

The boy took out a form and read it. "American Literature 1, Section 1003."

"Why do you want to study American Literature? Are you deeply interested in the culture of your country?"

"It fits into my schedule, and I need another core class for graduation. So my advisor put me down for your class," he answered without a trace of irony.

"There are plenty of core classes."

"All that are left open are at eight a.m.," the boy said in explanation, "Yours is at twelve thirty. I don't do well with early classes. They don't fit in with my learning style."

"But eight a.m. is a wonderful time to take a class. You can get up early, have breakfast, go to class, and still be out in plenty of time to prepare for your other classes, or the rest of your day. I'm usually up by six myself, but then people say that I don't have a life, and, to be honest, I sometimes have to agree." Gil smiled at the young man who didn't seem to quite know how to take him.

"But you have to sign this so I can take your class."

"No. Not really. You see, they call it an *overload* because it means I have enough students already; my quota is filled, so to speak. I have enough student widgets on my particular assembly line, so I don't have to let anyone else in at all. In fact, I fervently hope each night before I go to bed that some of my students will *drop* my course, most of them, if possible. Now if I let you in because of your, at best, very lame reason, namely that you can't get yourself out of bed in time for a class before noon, then I have to let others in my class who might have somewhat less lame reasons, like they have to work in order to afford to go to school."

"I have a work study job in the library," the boy said brightly.

"That's very good," Gil replied, "So then you'll be raring to go right after your eight o'clock class. See how well that works out for you?" After receiving no response, he added, "Now, you take it easy. Have a nice productive semester. Please do try to learn something while you're here; it's really your last, best hope." Gil resumed reading the book in his lap, and the boy, looking bemused, left.

Gil's phone rang. "Doctor Sykes," he said absentmindedly.

"Gil?"

"Valerie? How are you? I was going to call but didn't know your schedule."

"I'm fine, just wondering if you're going to the conference in Chicago in November."

"I planned on it. Not presenting or anything, but I will be going. Why?"

"No real reason. I have a paper on something you might find interesting. I can email it to you if you like."

"You mean you want my input, Val?"

"Please?" She sounded relieved. "I'm stuck, and I need help. You're one of the few who can actually see what I'm trying to do. But I'm afraid that there'll be a lot of angry people when I'm finished." She waited a moment, and then asked, "Have you ever heard of black pirates in colonial times?"

"No. I never heard of any black pirates, and of course it would seem silly to call them African-Americans in the eighteenth century."

"Well, they existed, and they formed pirate compacts, or Charters. Often, they'd sail on behalf of a European power, France, England, or Spain. Some of them were escaped slaves, others were free black men." She paused, and her voice shifted to a lower register, as if she didn't want to be heard. "I found something out that's kind of shocking. Your input would mean a lot to me. It can have serious ramifications, and the fact that I happen to be an African-American woman will give certain people even more reason to hate me."

"I'm glad to help. After I read it, we can have lunch," Gil said. The prospect of seeing what she'd discovered excited him. That era had been his first area of interest, and, as much as he liked Melville and the Transcendentalists, he really had a better background in Colonial America. He'd become the "American Literature Professor" after the previous one retired and the college never got around to replacing him. Now he only taught Colonial Literature about once every other year, only when enough English majors including graduate students expressed an interest, which was getting rarer.

"I appreciate it," Valerie said. "How are things going there at Bradbury College? Have you started up yet?"

"Yes, we started today, and I'll be here until the day I die—or retire, whichever comes first." He took a breath and sipped his coffee. "If you're referencing the first week in the desperate battle to hold back the next Dark Age, we're losing, badly I'm afraid. The Cantons have fallen to the barbarians with their smart phones and other such enhanced microchips; they will be here soon. As a matter of fact, the trustees are meeting today in order to decide if we surrender completely to the barbarians or try to maintain one last stronghold of academic integrity. My guess is that it's a hands-down capitulation. There will be some talk of productivity, student retention, and number of widgets graduated per professor. It's all beyond me."

"Same old Gil." Valerie chuckled. "I'm sure you will set them straight."

"Of course, but they never listen, not to me anyway. How are things at Chamberlain?"

"About the same. In fact, I have to get ready for a class. Bye, Gil. I'll email the paper to you. It hasn't been proofread yet, just so you know."

"That's not a problem," Gil said. "You take care, Valerie."

"You, too."

Gil stared at his desk phone, thinking how almost no one called him anymore; usually it was an email or maybe a text on his cell. As if it read his mind and wanted to prove him wrong, the telephone rang.

"Hello," Gil said, without his usual greeting.

"Gil?"

"Marion? Sorry, I left so early this morning that I forgot to wake you."

"That's fine, I heard you leave. Got a call from Richard, actually it's from Claudia about Richard" she said, almost apologetically. Richard was their nephew and had always been what was euphemistically referred to as "troubled" years ago. Gil frequently remarked that, "Before we were all politically correct, he would have been called an asshole." Claudia, Richard's mother, was Marion's younger sister, and had turned to Gil and Marion when her husband had died in a car accident just when Richard was entering high school. At least once a month, she reached out for help.

Gil and Marion often discussed that one of Richard's biggest problems was Claudia, who could be unusually gullible when it came to believing the latest unbelievable reason why Richard had not really been guilty of the infraction he'd been charged with, from fighting with another student when he was in school—"*He* started it. I was just walking down the hall—to his many DWI charges—"The test equipment wasn't properly calibrated, Mom. I had, like, one drink all night. No way I was drunk."

"What's up?" Gil was almost afraid to ask.

"The usual, I'm afraid. He stole someone's car—one of his friend's, actually. He took it without permission and got stopped at a roadblock. Aggravated unlicensed driving and DWI, not to mention car theft."

"Oh, crap."

"And, Gil? This time they're talking about jail, very seriously talking about jail."

Gil could imagine the look of strain on her face from the tone in her voice. The last judge had made it clear that the next time he messed up, Richard was going to jail.

"I'm not sure there's anything we can do. We lent your sister a ton of money for the last attorney," Gil said. It hadn't really been a loan. Claudia had no way of paying it back, not on her income. They referred to it that way in order to spare her feelings.

"I know." Marion sighed. "It's just that Claudia's beside herself."

"She spends a lot of time there, beside herself, mostly because of Richard. I don't think jail is the answer, but I have no idea what else to do. Our own kids are costing us enough right now. I can't jeopardize their education because of their idiot cousin."

"No one's asking you to do any such thing. My sister just needs someone to talk to." Marion's anger flashed.

"Sorry, that was thoughtless. It's just that Mary and Jason are on my mind right now, both in school and all. Jason's just in his first year."

"I know that. They're my kids, too."

"Yes, they are. I can bear witness to that. I was there, both times. Still have the scars where you dug into my arm instead of the bedpost." He smiled. "Unless they mixed them up afterwards, they're definitely your kids." He laughed. "Now, we men have to take that whole thing on little bit of faith you know."

"You certainly do," Marion agreed, her good humor restored. Then, hesitantly, she said, "I've invited Claudia over for dinner tonight. She was so lost, I didn't know what else to do."

"Okay. Should I get something to drink, maybe an extra-large bottle of wine?"

"Good idea, Gil."

"Okay, so I'll be fine. What should I get for you and Claudia to drink?"

"Bye, sweetie," Marion said with plenty of irony.

"Bye, honey." He hung up the phone. "I guess you really screwed the pooch this time you spoiled little brat," he said out loud, and tried to remember the name of the criminal defense attorney he'd hired only last year.

*\*\**

The second large bottle of wine was almost empty, and Claudia had drunk her share of both. They were sitting at the round oak table in Gil and Marion's house, the one they'd picked up at an auction right after they were married. Marion had refinished it, after waiting two years for Gil to get around to it. Marion had thrown together a salad to go with the lasagna, and Gil had gotten a couple of bottles of a Tuscan red. Gil eyed the contents of the bottle, and quickly poured it in his class. Marion gave him a dirty look, and he shrugged his shoulders. Claudia didn't seem to notice. She was involved in the long narrative that she'd repeated in one form or another all night long. Gil was losing patience.

"I can't believe his friend lied like that. He let Richard borrow his car, and then said he'd stolen it. And Richard said that the police didn't do the breathalyzer right, and that their equipment was off. It probably hasn't been calibrated in years. The blood test was bogus, too." She stopped and took a long pull of wine, then looked around for the bottle. Gil had taken the empty off the table.

"That could be true," Gil said, trying hard not to sound too sarcastic, "but maybe you could explain the other DWI for me? This isn't the first time he's had issues with alcohol. Luckily, this time he got stopped before he could do any damage." He took a breath. "And when he totaled his car last year, did the tree jump out into the middle of the road?"

"No, of course not," Claudia said indignantly. "I told you. He fell asleep from studying too hard."

Gil covered his face to keep from smiling, also knowing Marion was determining the right angle to kick him under the table. He knew he was on dangerous ground and would have dropped the whole thing except for the total cluelessness of his sister-in-law.

"It's really your fault, too, Gil," she said.

"What? In what way?" She didn't hear the dangerous calm in his voice.

"You got him into school and put him in a program that was over his head. He exhausted himself, pure and simple."

"He was taking first-year classes, for god's sake. They're essentially 'welcome to college courses.'" Gil slammed his glass on the table and ignored Marion's look that pleaded with him to let it go. "Richard is a liar and a punk. If you believe one word of what you just said to us, then you're a goddamned imbecile. He took the car from his buddy without his permission, unless his buddy is stupid enough to let someone who lost his license take his car. Then he got drunk and got caught at a roadblock because he didn't have the sense to turn around. Thank your lucky stars he didn't end up smashing this car up, too. The insurance company would probably have bailed because *Richard has no license and was drunk*. So Richard would have been liable, which means *you* would have been liable for the car. Thank goodness he got caught and he didn't have a chance to make it worse." He took a breath but didn't wait for her to respond. "For your information, the police know how to administer a breathalyzer test; that's what they do for a living, and his blood test was conclusive. What was it? Almost three times the legal limit—again? Defense lawyers are supposed to question the calibration of the breathalyzer, because *that's what they do*. Their job is to generate plausible doubt, although that would be a hell of a task in this case. Furthermore, Richard failed out of school because he never bothered showing up to his classes.

"He screwed up. Stop making excuses. It doesn't help him at all when you make excuses."

Claudia burst into tears. Marion looked like she was contemplating stabbing Gil with the knife she'd used to cut the lasagna. There was a long silence punctuated only by Claudia's sobs.

"You always have to be right, don't you?" Marion whispered in his ear as she grabbed Gil's plate and silverware. She started stacking the dishes and clearing the table. "Anyone for cheesecake and coffee? I also have decaf," she said, forcing a smile.

# Chapter 2

Marion Sykes went to bed still a little angry with Gil. However, he had patched things up with Claudia, and she had left in better spirits than she'd been in at the end of dinner and was also relatively sober after coffee and cake. Marion knew what the problem was, and she knew that Gil was right. Absolutely right, in fact. Richard had played on the untimely death of his father for all it was worth. School administrators, police officers, probation officers had all cut him slack because his father had died tragically, unexpectedly. One day he'd said goodbye and gone to work. He never came back. While he was driving home on the highway, a metal rod had flown off a truck that was in front of him and smashed through his windshield hitting him in the head. No eyewitness could remember exactly what the truck had looked like or who it might have belonged to. Other than some life insurance from work, there was no other money, so Claudia had to get a job, which made things worse because Richard was left on his own. He learned quickly that invoking his father's accident would get him a fair distance when it came to avoiding punishment, and he also was smart enough to use this to play at least some of the therapists and counselors.

Marion went to bed late, finding Gil already asleep, these thoughts about her nephew swirling around in her head, competing with worry about a deadline that was now pressing because she had only worked a couple of hours that morning. She had been a freelance editor for a few years now, and hated being interrupted on deadline, but liked the work. It was better for her than driving to Manhattan and working for a publisher, which she had done for several years. The twenty-hour a week commute had gotten too much. When Gil got a permanent appointment at Bradbury, she went freelance.

Eventually, her thoughts stilled, and she drifted off.

When she woke at her usual six a.m., she quietly slipped out of bed to let Gil sleep another hour and went to the kitchen to make coffee. She heard Gil get out of bed a few minutes later.

"You didn't sleep very well last night," he said, sipping the coffee she'd poured for him. It wasn't a question.

"Had too much on my mind."

"Sorry."

"It wasn't your fault. I know I was mad at you, but you were right. Someone had to tell her. Not that I think it will do any good at all."

"I can find that attorney's business card. You know, the one we used last time. For the life of me, I can't remember his name. But I can't give him a retainer. That will have to come from Claudia."

"It was McMasters I think, or something like that. The card should be in our address book. But she doesn't have it. No money at all for that. She barely makes thirty a year at that place she works."

"After all these years? That's pretty low. Isn't she a manager of some sort?"

"Yep. She gets a raise every time the minimum wage goes up. Sometimes they give a small bonus if her section beats their quota."

"That's sad."

"Welcome to retail sales. The owners of the chain store are all billionaires, upper management brings down million-dollar bonuses, but everyone else makes minimum or a maybe just a little above."

"Nice little scam. Good old American business, and if the people complain, they get fired, or their job gets moved to China," Gil commented. "We are really at our limit, though," he said thoughtfully. "I can't see how we can help her this time."

"Let's not worry about it right now," Marion said. Gil finished his coffee and made his way to his bathroom. Since the kids had gone, he'd taken over their bathroom; she still used the one off their bedroom. It was a while before he emerged dressed for work, kissed her and left.

"I'll call before I leave to see if we need anything from the store," he said.

Marion finished her coffee and sat at her laptop. She was working on a book that exhaustively studied the three-toed sloth. Apparently, very little was actually known about the creatures, and the author had spent a few years traveling in Central and South America observing and helping with retuning orphans to the wild. The adults were easily killed on roads and highways, so there was a problem with orphaned baby sloths. Marion learned more than she'd ever imagined about their sex lives, eating habits, and the fact that the three-toed sloth could swim, while the two-toed preferred to live in trees. While the book was full of information, like most scientists, the author could not write interesting prose. She dubbed these books "two-toothpick-books" because she claimed she needed to prop open both eyes with toothpicks in order to be able to edit them without falling asleep. She had gotten a lot of them lately, and suspected it was because she was the only one who would take them.

She'd left off at: Sloths copulate for around twenty-five minutes, although they have been observed doing so for much longer, and somewhat shorter, intervals. Marion had the image of a dysentery-skinny man in jungle camouflage, wearing a pith helmet, sweat soaking through

19

his clothes in the tropical wet heat, holding a stopwatch and carefully observing two young adult sloths making more sloths. The image made her smile as she worked on the book, fixing errors and making dense prose less so, or at least making the voice less passive.

She'd been working for a couple of hours when the phone rang. It was Claudia. Marion didn't pick up, but Claudia was the queen of leaving long, convoluted, involved messages on phone mail, and, after listening to her for as long as she could stand, Marion gave up. It took Claudia a while to realize that she wasn't talking to an answering machine.

"Claudia? Claudia, it's me. I just got in the door when I heard you leaving a message. What's up?"

"They're going to arraign him today. I don't know what to do." She sounded almost hysterical.

"You have to have him plead not guilty, for one," Marion said. "This is not his first rodeo, and they'll probably charge him with a felony again, so there might be bail."

"We don't have an attorney."

"I know," Marion said. There was a long pause, neither sister saying anything. "He might have to go with the public defender this time." Marion said. "They will set bail."

"I have no money for that, either."

"You might have to get a bond if it's too high." Marion tried to comfort her by saying, "We can maybe help a little. No one wants to see him in jail."

"I hate to ask you for anything. You've been so generous," Claudia said, starting to sob again.

"Sorry we can't help even more." Marion thought for a second. "What about his father's relatives? Have you kept in touch at all?"

"They're nice people, and we exchange cards at Christmas, but they don't have any money."

"Sorry."

"It's not your fault," Claudia said, but the tone in her voice sounded accusatory, as if somehow it *was* Marion's fault, as if somehow Claudia expected her to help out—no, not expected, but *required* it. As if Claudia felt that Marion and Gil had an obligation to support their nephew every time his asinine and inexcusable behavior got him in trouble, as if simply sharing some genes placed an unyielding obligation on them.

"No, it's not our fault at all," Marion said in clipped tones.

"Why are you mad?"

"I'm not mad, but I'm a little busy. I'm late for my deadline."

"Sorry, this has me on edge."

"It has all of us on edge," Marion said. "Call me after he's arraigned.

We'll try to come up with a plan after that." She didn't wait for her sister to say anything before she hung up the phone. She looked at it for a minute, and then unplugged it and went back to work.

*** 

Gil stopped at the local grocery store on his way home as he often did. It was easier for him to stop on his way home than for her to interrupt her work to leave the house and go back. Gil went through the aisles, picking up the few items they needed.

"Gil?" He heard his name from behind him and turned to see Christina, a friend who he knew had been working on a divorce, and who had a young boy that she was getting custody of. Gil took a minute to recognize her; she had lost some weight, and her body looked muscular.

"Christina. I didn't recognize you."

"I've been working out. It's my new religion."

"You look healthy," Gil said, although he thought she had an odd strained appearance, like her muscles were pushing hard against skin, making the veins and sinews seem unnecessarily taught. He wondered if she might be taking some sort of steroid, then wondered if women actually took steroids, other than Russian Olympic athletes.

"How've you been? I think that the last time I saw you was at a holiday party at Paige and Josh's house." Gil wasn't being politically correct. At Paige and Josh's it was indeed a "holiday party." He was a secular Jew, and she was raised as a Wiccan. Jesus was not at all a part of their metaphysical makeup, so celebrating Christmas really made no sense, although they always had a beautiful tree. Paige made all the ornaments.

"I think so. That was last year. There probably won't be a party this year. Paige and Josh broke up. He has a girlfriend, and she moved in with an old boyfriend."

"Really?" Gil was surprised.

"Yes. They had their problems. Didn't you notice the strain at the last party? Probably not; you and Marion seem to always be in your own world." She smiled, and it looked a little like a grimace. "How is she anyway? Marion?"

"Good. She's been getting a lot of work lately. You know how it goes with her, feast or famine." Gil couldn't believe he'd just used such a cliché, but the truth was that Christina always made him a little nervous. She was very attractive, and at that last party they'd spent a lot of time together because Marion had vanished for a couple of hours after latching on to some friends, leaving him alone.

"Nice to hear that she's working. Not everyone is so lucky," Christina said.

"How about yourself?"

"Oh, I have my same old job at Bradbury, in the vice provost's office, but I'm trying to start a new business." She dug in her pocketbook and handed him a beautiful business card sporting a generic figure of a body. "I finally got my certification as a massage therapist, and I took one of the spare rooms in my home and set it all up. You remember me talking about it at that party?"

"Yes, I do," Gil replied. It was one of the many things they had talked about. He remembered she'd seemed very excited about it. She'd needed another few months to certify and had also mentioned losing weight because she felt that no one would trust an overweight massage therapist. So she had achieved her goals.

Gil felt a sudden depression. If anything, he was pretty much at the same point where he had been at that party almost a year ago. He was still working at Bradbury, Marion was still doing the same job, his kids were now both in school, and he remembered bending her ear about his idiot nephew Richard and his clueless sister-in-law. He seemed to be stuck in the same place in time.

"How are your kids?" she asked.

"They're both fine. Jason started at Albany State this year, and Mary's in her last year on a track scholarship at UCLA."

"The scholarship must be a big help."

"Yes, but there still are plenty of bills not covered, and Bradbury isn't much help if your kids don't go there." He had forgotten that she worked at the same place.

"Don't I know it. My boy still has some time before he's ready for college."

"It'll go by quicker than you think."

"What about that nephew of yours, has he straightened up? I remember you talking about him at the party."

"He's okay, I guess. Really haven't heard much about him."

"We'll that's good news, then. Sorry, but I've got to get going. Be sure to tell all of your friends about my business. You should come yourself." She started to turn, then stopped. "The way you're slumped over, I know that your shoulders must hurt. I can take care of that in a half-hour session." She went behind him and put her fingertips on the back of his shoulders and worked the muscles for a short while. He felt them loosen, and his head went up. "See?" she said. "Already you're an inch taller." She worked his shoulder muscles a little more and then stopped. He moved his head around with a range of motion that he hadn't had for what felt like weeks. "The first one is free, but you'll have to pay for the rest." She smiled at him again, but this time it didn't look at all like a grimace.

Gil put her business card in his wallet.

*\*\**

"Still slaving away, I see," said Gil as he walked into the kitchen with a bag of groceries. Although they had converted a spare room into an office for her, Marion would often end up working on the dining room table. She preferred to spread her papers and reference books out, and she also liked the light in the dining room because of the skylight. It didn't make a glare across the computer screen.

"Almost done," she said, not looking up.

"With the book? Or just with today's pages?"

"The book," she said. "And ahead of deadline."

"Wow. You'll probably miss reading about your friends the sloths."

"Nope."

"Don't be too hasty. You and those sloths have become closer than you care to admit, I'm sure." Gil couldn't resist teasing her a little. "Anyway, a new book on the way?"

"No. They said things are slow, will have to wait a little for another book, nothing in the pipeline."

"You should take a break anyway. You've been under the gun for a few months now with all those deadlines."

"That's true," she said. "How are things going? How did the semester start?"

"So far, it's pretty typical, nothing too crazy. Already have too many meetings."

"Sorry."

"Comes with the territory. Meetings are the bane of education." He went to the bedroom and changed his clothes. It was time for a walk; he liked to walk around the neighborhood. Just walk. Not power walking, not with weights, no music, no fancy gear. He liked to say that he just walked the way humans have walked for two hundred thousand years, putting one foot in front of the other and trying not to fall over or bump into anything. He took a left out of his driveway and started for the park, then walked through the wooded field at the end of the housing project, and doubled back again through the park around the playground. Several young mothers were in the park watching their kids play on the outdoor gym that the neighborhood had built after what seemed like an interminable fund-raiser. Gil had been touched for a donation several times before he finally had gently told them to find another willing donor. After the park it was a quick walk back to his front door.

"Your timing is perfect."

"You mean dinner is ready?"

"No. I mean that just after you left, Claudia called."

"And?"

"They set Richard's bail at twenty-five thousand dollars."

"Really? Did he kill someone we don't know about?"

"No. The judge apparently recognized him," Marion said.

"Wow."

"She can put up a twenty-five-hundred-dollar bond. The attorney said that she'd get most of it back after all of this is finished."

"She hired an attorney?"

"No. Richard is considered to be financially independent at his age, so he got a public defender."

"Oh," Gil said as he took off his walking shoes near the door and put on some slippers. They were both very quiet for a few minutes. Marion had already poured a glass of wine. Gil joined her.

"She's going to have to borrow the money from us," Marion said.

"I know," Gil replied. "I already went to the bank. You can write her a check tomorrow."

# Chapter 3

Right before he left for the day, Gil noticed an email from Valerie; her paper was attached. He quickly printed it out, found a paperclip in his desk, and tossed the paper into his briefcase. Since it was Friday, he'd try to get to it sometime over the weekend. When he got home, there was a note on the table. Marion had gone to Claudia's, and they were going out to dinner later that evening. Gil wondered why Marion still left notes when everyone else in the country simply sent text messages. He'd half expected it; since she'd finished the latest project, she'd have to devote some time to Claudia. As the eldest sister in the family, Marion was the surrogate mother to most of her siblings, but especially to Claudia, the youngest.

Gil warmed up some leftovers for supper and sat in front of the television. tuning to a major network for the news. When it got too insipid—the newscasters were trying to come up with another adjective than "cute" for the obligatory "adorable video" segment—he browsed the channels for a while, but Friday night television was too much of a wasteland, and he wasn't in the mood for streaming a movie, so he picked up a novel he'd begun a few days before and read for a couple of hours. It was just interesting enough to keep his attention and distract him. He hadn't been happy about digging into his savings—yet again—for Richard, but Marion wouldn't have forgiven him for letting their nephew go to jail, even though the boy still might end up there. It all depended on the DA and the judge, neither of whom had looked pleased to see Richard again.

It was late when Marion came home. He heard her car alarm chirp when she locked the door, and then her step on the porch. She had her key in her hand, but Gil had left the door open. He'd lock it if he went to bed while she was still out.

"Oh, you're still up?"

"Yeah, it's Friday."

"Oh, right. Working at home makes me forget that there is a weekend."

"My students began the weekend yesterday."

"We did, too, when we were that age."

"Not me." Gil smiled.

"Nonsense," Marion said. "I was there, remember?"

"I don't remember much from that era. What was your name again?

Did we sleep together?"

"No. Never," Marion said as she opened the fridge.

"I thought you said you two were going out to eat," Gil said.

"My mistake, I forgot who invited me," Marion said while pulling plastic containers out and putting food on a microwave plate.

"You mean?"

"Dino pizza with a coupon?" she asked. "Yep. I should have known better." Dino Pizza was probably the worst pizza in the state. The only reason it was in business at all was that it was attached to an arcade where kids played video games As a way to get customers in the pizzeria, they gave deep discount coupons, so the pizza actually cost less than it cost them to make, a loss leader, the idea being that customers would spend enough at the arcade to make up for it. Claudia was a regular. Gilbert had eaten there once and refused to ever go back.

"We talked about everything but Richard," Marion said while waiting for her food to heat up.

"I'm surprised you could talk about anything," Gil said.

"It was tough. We sat as far from the arcade as we could, but my ears are still ringing." She pulled the plate out of the microwave, set up a TV table, and turned on the news. They talked for a while, and then Marion went to bed. Gil wasn't sleepy, but he didn't want to watch TV or continue to read the novel. He looked at his briefcase and remembered Val's paper. "Might as well get started," he mumbled. He took the paper out of his briefcase, grabbed a pencil, sat on the couch and began to read, making an occasional note. At four a.m., he crawled into bed.

They had no plans for Saturday, so he and Marion went out for a drive. Life had been stressful, and they hoped a visit to Sommers Lake might be a restful way to spend the day. The weather had turned warm, and it was a sunny late summer day. They paid the admission fee, parked in the lot, and then went to the beach. A few people were swimming, but it was already late in the season and the water was cold. Technically, the beach was closed after Labor Day.

It wasn't too long before Gil got bored, so he asked Marion if she wanted to take a short hike. They put the folding chairs in the car, and Gil picked up a small daypack. They took the long trail to a lookout point they liked. It was a few miles through the woods, so it usually had far fewer people than the shorter trail that went directly to the escarpment. They went off the trail at a point they knew well and emerged at a promontory, where they both sat on a ledge overlooking the valley and the Hudson River. People had carved their initials into the shale ledge; some carvings were over 100 years old. *Meghan and William, 1898* had carved their names in a heart. William must have been pretty strong, and very much in love, to carve so deeply into the rock that it was still clear after all those years. Gil and Marion always looked for the heart whenever they hiked to that spot.

"Look, Meghan and William," Marion said.

"Yep. Still here," Gil said.

"I wonder what happened to them. I wonder if they were married when they carved that heart."

"No. They were still in love," Gilbert said.

"Spoil sport." She looked him in the eye. "Is that how you feel about us?"

"No," he said, and put his arm around her. They sat in silence for a long while, listening to the quiet sounds of the day. "I like it here, but I want to get away. I mean really get away. I wonder, though, if that's possible, without changing our phone numbers and leaving no forwarding address. It would be too easy for people to find us any other way."

"Can't do it," Marion said. "And we'd have to at least get in touch with our kids."

"I know. Interesting idea, though."

"Something's bothering you," she said. "Is it Richard?"

"No. Not him, but, yes, something *is* on my mind," he said. "It can wait." He kissed her, and then again, and started to caress her, pushing gently against her blouse. She pulled back. "It's okay, we're married," he said.

"We're also in public," she replied. "What if someone comes up the trail?"

"No one uses this trail; they all take the easy route to the old Mountain House site. We can go under the ledge," Gil said, stroking her and kissing her on the neck. Gradually she relaxed and gave in.

"It will be damp under there," she said.

"That's why I brought my pack," he replied. "I have a blanket." She smiled. *You would think of that.* He stood and led her to the small recess under the outcropping. It wasn't their first time there. In fact, they had camped there in a small tent just before they were married. Marion wondered if William and Meghan had done the same thing on a warm late summer's day over a century ago; perhaps that's why the heart was cut so deeply into the stone.

On the way home, they stopped at a local diner for a late lunch. It had changed ownership since the last time they'd been there, and the food had been updated. Gil was a little disappointed at first, as he usually ordered the meatloaf. The food was now more contemporary pub-style food. He ordered a burger with porcini mushrooms and asiago cheese with truffle fries, and Marion ordered a salad with grilled seafood and grilled vegetables.

"You going to tell me what's on your mind?" Marion asked.

"Okay," Gil said, then took a bite of his sandwich. He picked up a fry, inhaled the smell of the truffles, and then slowly ate it. "I read Valerie's paper last night while you were asleep. I just wanted to get a quick idea of what she was writing about." Marion nodded. "Well, it looks as if she found out something that will really piss off a lot of people." He ate another fry before continuing. "It seems that the Declaration of Independence, at least some of the more famous parts of it, might not have been written at all by the man we thought wrote it."

"Really?"

"Yes. It seems that she has evidence that a pirate by the name of Jean the Mulatto wrote the most famous lines in the Charter of Agreement he had with his men. Jefferson simply plagiarized them."

"Such as?" Marion asked

"All men are created equal, for one."

"Wow."

# Chapter 4

Gil looked out over the amphitheater-style classroom. In spite of his campaign to scare away as many students at possible, he'd ended up with about as many as he'd started with. As students dropped the class, others stepped in. Even some hair-curling reviews by former students posted on an online teacher rating website didn't keep them away. He sighed and sized up the students, looking to see how many of the students seemed to understand that they were in a class that was about to begin, and how many were looking around or fiddling with their cell phones or electronics. He noted the students who seemed to understand what was expected of them had books out and were looking in his general direction, and also noted those who seemed to have no clue. Gil smiled at the students looking at him and began.

"We begin this class with *Moby Dick* by Herman Melville. You might have noticed that sometimes the title *Moby-Dick* is hyphenated. This is something that people did in 1851. We don't hyphenate this way anymore.

"It might not prove to be your most favorite book. There are no vampires, nor are there any zombies or angst-ridden child wizards, but Melville still managed to write a reasonably suspenseful book without them. There will be passages in this book that you will probably not understand, and that's why I'm here, but basically, I think you're probably too young to understand them anyway. The reading schedule is not terribly difficult, but you need to have your pages read before you get here. Sitting in the back of the room and reading, doing homework for another class, texting, or using your cell phone will count as an absence."

He stopped talking for a moment and noticed that some of the students in the back of the room were still texting and hadn't heard a word he'd said. He took roll, and then passed out the attendance sign-up sheet. He always took attendance. It was also a good way to help him learn their names.

"Anyway, let's get started. Does anyone have any questions about the assigned readings?" A girl with multicolored hair sitting in the first row put up her hand. Gil noticed that she looked very young, even for a freshman.

"Yes?"

"I read the chapters, but have trouble understanding Queegueg. Why is he in bed with Ishmael? I mean literally in bed?"

"Yeah. Are they gay or something?" A young man piped up.

"It shows Ishmael's naiveté," Gil responded. "While there is a lot of homoerotic subtext in this book, the average nineteenth-century reader would not have come to that conclusion. He would simply think that Ishmael was poor, and a bit naïve for renting half a bed in the first place, or that the tavern owner was being unscrupulous. But Ishmael might not have had a lot of choice. Like I said, he had very little money and was looking to ship out on a whaler, probably the equivalent of someone working as a roughneck on an oil rig or an oil tanker today. It was very hard work, but also good money. Even the three-hundredth share he is eventually offered could be more than the yearly income of most men at the time if they took in a lot of whale oil. Queequeg will be offered a ninetieth share because he is an excellent shot with the harpoon."

"You mean they could do that? Rent half your bed to someone else?" Another girl said.

"That's disgusting," said someone else. "He was supposed to be a cannibal, too, Queegueg."

"Yes," Gil said, "only he mentioned that his enemies gave him indigestion. He never embraced cannibalism with any real gusto."

A few students laughed, catching on to his humor, others looked confused, and a few were still texting.

Gil continued. "The inn was crowded, and it was sometimes a practice to split a bed between two patrons. As Ishmael put it, 'better to sleep with a sober cannibal than a drunken Christian.'"

"I still think it's all disgusting," said the same student.

*At least she actually read it.*

The student who had opened the discussion—Edith Frank, he discovered, reading the class roster—spoke up.

"He didn't really want to sail on a whaler, though. He really wanted adventure, but he had no money. I really liked that first paragraph where he was talking about being alone and being depressed and without money, and how he was going to sail away to avoid committing suicide. His reference to Cato the Younger is pretty clear, not to mention that he went to sea as a substitute for 'pistol and ball.' He needed to get away. He didn't trust himself staying there and getting even more depressed," she said with an authority beyond her years.

"Right! Did any of you realize that he might be contemplating suicide at the start of the novel?" Several students raised their hands. Gil was delighted.

"Some have argued that he wasn't contemplating real suicide, but more of a metaphysical suicide, or perhaps a figure of speech when we say in exasperation 'I'm going to kill myself if I don't get that job'. But his reference to Cato is pretty clear. Do you know that story?" A couple of students raised their hands. Gil was impressed; most high schools had long since cut out much history of the Roman Empire.

"The story is that Cato the Younger, rather than subject himself to the rule of Julius Caesar, who was about to become the first Emperor of Rome and bring about the end of the Roman Republic, stabbed himself to death. There are graphic eyewitness accounts from his servants who rushed into his bedroom when they heard the noise of him falling over. He chose death rather than live under an absolute dictator. It certainly is an interesting way for Melville to start the book. Even the first line, 'Call me Ishmael' has become a classic in itself. Notice he doesn't say 'my name is Ishmael,' but 'call me Ishmael.'"

"The first paragraphs are more like a poem than prose," someone said.

"There is also some irony in that first paragraph, a comment on the need for money," Edith offered.

"Exactly. The book is full of irony on many levels. Melville really challenges the cultural norms of nineteenth-century America, and the trek we all must make through life." Gil said. He felt a little guilty about being so hard on them at the beginning. He was pleased with this group, although the usual number of them were surprised by the fact that a popular chain of coffee shops was named after the stoic Quaker who was first mate of the Pequod. Gil used that to gauge the reactions of the various students: if they showed surprise, then he found out who actually read the book from those who were faking it by saying a lot of noncommittal drivel.

This group seemed genuinely animated and curious. *It might turn out to be a decent semester yet.* Gil was always surprised at the different personalities the classes could have. Some were so quiet and reserved they made him wonder if he was doing any good at all, but occasionally he got enough serious students to make it worthwhile, and that reminded him of why he'd chosen this career in the first place.

When he got to his office, he sipped what coffee was left in his thermos, and looked at the calendar. He had a meeting coming up in a half hour, so he took his lunch out of the refrigerator in the faculty kitchen and ate a sandwich in his office in front of his PC, checking the news online. It was a quiet day. Sometimes it seemed to him that the start of the school year was a trigger for natural or manmade disasters that could dominate the news for weeks. Something about the first two weeks in September seemed prone to disasters. Except for the usual mayhem, such as run-of-the-mill murders, and minor terrorist assaults in third-world countries, countries that didn't weigh heavily in the U.S. world and national news, nothing else was going on.

When the time came, he went to the small seminar room reserved for meetings; most of the others were there. He still couldn't figure out how he'd gotten on the ad hoc committee for campus safety and security. He'd managed to duck most committee work for the past few years and guessed his luck had run out. His appointment to the committee might have had something to do with the short opinion piece he'd written for the local newspaper after the latest shooting massacre in a college not far from them.

So far, the committee had advised the college to be sure all the classroom phones were working—a surprising number had been found to be out of order or simply turned off—that the room number of each room be stenciled on the inside of the classrooms, and that the doors have locks. Gil had found it surprising that almost none of the classrooms in many of the older buildings had locks on their doors.

Now they'd moved on to other forms of threats to safety. The scheduled presentation for this meeting was on bombs. Gil and the others were listening to a very earnest young man in a uniform who was talking about the dangers of homemade pipe bombs. It seemed they were ridiculously easy to make, and triggering mechanisms could include anything from a fuse, like those used for fireworks, to a cell phone. The presenter had models that he passed around the table, and a very professional-looking slide show with videos and animation.

When he finished, Gil felt that they should applaud.

"So what do you propose we do to deal with this threat?" Millie Cavanaugh, a business professor, asked. Gil wasn't surprised; she was at least as earnest as the young man.

"Well, for one," he said, "you need to practice bomb drills in your classrooms."

"Yes," Millie said in agreement.

"What exactly do you mean?" Gil asked.

"You need to instruct your students to leave the building if there is a bomb reported."

"So they get the day off then?" Gil said. "My guess is that finals week we will get a lot of bombers flocking to campus."

Millie stared daggers at Gil.

"No, not the whole day. We will quickly sweep the building with trained dogs to find if there are any explosives."

"How often have you actually found explosives when a bomb was reported?" Gil asked out of genuine curiosity, although he was sure everyone else in the room thought he was being difficult.

"Not any, yet." He seemed disappointed.

"None?"

"We did find a bunch of fireworks in the high school last spring," he said.

"Oh," Gil said. "So what happens if you do find a bomb?"

"Now that is where things get very serious." The young man brightened.

"I would imagine so," Gil said, and was happy that Millie, unlike his wife, wouldn't dream of kicking him under the table—at least he didn't think so.

"We then move the people back to a perimeter of a hundred feet, and then the bomb squad comes in to defuse the bomb."

"How long do they take?" Gil asked.

"To defuse the bomb?"

"No," Gil said. "To get here in the first place."

"They are stationed in Greenmills."

"That's thirty minutes away," Gil said. "Assuming you find the bomb quickly and then we wait for the bomb squad. My guess is they're not just sitting around, and it will take some time for them to gather. And by the time they arrive here, we're talking about at least an hour?" The man nodded.

"I guess," Gil said, "we can give the added instruction to 'plug your ears in case of an explosion.' What do you think, Millie?"

"I think this is a serious matter," Millie said.

"I do, too," Gil replied. "There seems to be no end to the crazies out there who want to hurt total strangers for reasons mostly confined to their sick and depraved imaginations, but we can only do so much. If we start having bomb drills, I can assure you that at least one of the less mature Neanderthals who populate some of our classes will get the bright idea to call in a bomb threat so he can go back to bed and sleep off his hangover without worrying about getting in trouble for missing class or possibly avoiding a test."

"Gil has a good point," Dean Malone said. She was sitting in on this meeting because it was the first of the year. She would have no time in her schedule once the semester got underway. Gary Sime, the Assistant Vice Provost was also there. He came to meetings from time to time, but usually didn't say much.

"But won't that leave our kids defenseless?" Millie said.

"Not really," the dean said. "If we get a bomb threat, we can simply set off the fire alarm. Make it a long fire drill. The students will leave the building same as if it were for a fire. I'm sure the fire trucks will arrive anyway, and as long as no one knows what caused the alarm in the first place, we don't need to advertise it. Let everyone assume it was a fire. The point is to get the students out of the buildings. How we do it is not important." She stopped to clear her throat, then said, "Furthermore, it would discourage those calling in fake bomb threats because they won't get any publicity. If they say anything at all, we'll find out who they are."

"That makes sense," one of the other members of the committee said.

The matter was settled for everyone but Millie, but the meeting moved on to other business, which was every bit as serious as a bomb, only far more likely to happen. There had been some issues in the past with sexual assaults, but the previous year had brought two high profile cases, one involving a varsity basketball player, and the other involving a tenured professor. There had been much media time and ink spent on both events.

The only one who'd been surprised about the professor had been his wife. He'd gotten caught when his latest conquest, a first-year student, had confessed to her resident assistant in her dorm that the professor in question was going to leave his wife and marry her. The red flag in that romantic scenario was that the professor had also given the resident assistant the exact same line when she'd had an affair with him in *her* freshman year.

The R.A. reported it to the Dean of Students, and then what everyone had known for years about the professor became common public knowledge in every local newspaper and was picked up by the wire services, which, of course, meant that now *someone would have to do something about it.* Since he was close enough to retirement age, it was simple enough to fill out some papers, give him a quick wine and cheese party, and wish him well. He had broken the sexual harassment rules of the college, but since the girl was over eighteen, the sex was considered to be consensual, if somewhat unscrupulously solicited. The student found herself highly recommended for a more competitive liberal arts college farther up the Hudson and transferred the following semester.

The other issue, with the basketball player, however, was proving to be persistent, and far more serious. The coach had tried, very crudely, to cover things up, and the school had offered to internally adjudicate the case, but the young woman involved wouldn't have any part of it. It wasn't like she had been going out with the athlete and he had assaulted her on a date, although that would have been bad enough, and it would have given the conservative press an opening to blame the victim. She didn't know him and had only been at the same bar he had. Date rape drugs were suspected, but her blood test was inconclusive. On the other hand, the rape kit had produced damning evidence against the basketball player. Due to details discovered by the doctor, it was almost impossible for the sex to have been consensual. She had left school while the case was working its way through the criminal justice system, as had the athlete, and the school was trying to put some distance between it and the whole mess, but all three people were technically still part of the college, although the player was suspended and the coach was on paid leave.

While the committee couldn't make a binding decision, it did recommend that the basketball player be expelled from school pending the outcome of his case.

The coach was another issue, and the committee had no power over terminating his contract, but it was recommended that the college attorneys look into the possibility, and that his contract be terminated at once if legally possible in spite of the fact that several rich and influential members of the alumni had started a campaign to retain him.

The alleged victim had posted a video she'd made with her phone of the coach, dressed in his school warm-up jacket, threatening her if she didn't drop the charges. It had, at that moment, over three million hits.

Then it was recommended that the faculty handbook section on sexual harassment be emailed to all faculty and staff, and that the Student Life Office conduct mandatory sexual harassment seminars for the students.

"I don't think this goes far enough," one of the members commented after the vote, and most of the others agreed.

"What do you propose?" Dean Malone asked.

"If a sexual assault happens, it is illegal. We need to call the police. It should be their job to investigate. If we take it on with an internal investigation, then it looks like we're covering it up."

"Good point," Millie said.

"Yes and no," Gil said. "If we refer every alleged crime on this campus to the police, then we have to, by law, report it. It goes into our statistics. How many students would want to come here if it looked like our campus was crime-ridden? Do you think for a second that our competition reports all of their problems to the police? Two of them have campuses in large urban high-crime areas; my guess is that they keep a lot of information to themselves."

"They do wrong so we do the same?" Millie said.

"No, just that we need to be practical, too. These are kids we're dealing with. They screw up, sometimes very seriously," Gil said, thinking of his nephew.

"So we ignore rape?" Millie was upset.

"No. Absolutely not," Gil said, "but we don't trivialize it either. Not every unwise sexual encounter is rape. Sometimes it's just stupid."

"And I say let the police and the courts figure that out," Millie said.

"And I say that's a very bad idea. Have you ever dealt with the police or the courts? Not to mention that everything that happens on campus will now be published in the paper and made official. Do you really want that? I'm not saying cover up a criminal sexual assault, or any criminal activity, but referring every case to the local police department might backfire on us in ways we can't even think of now. I think that would be a very bad policy, but if the committee wants to recommend it, then I'll abstain."

There was some more debate, and the committee voted to recommend that the school adopt a policy of referring every case where a crime was suspected, especially sexual assault cases, to the local town police. Gil abstained as he had promised.

When Gil got back to his office, a student was waiting for him next to his door. He looked vaguely familiar, but Gil couldn't place him.

"Hi, Professor Sykes," the boy said.

"Hello. Are you waiting for me?"

"Yes."

"Well, come in, but I do have some reading to do before class."

"Okay." He followed Gil into the office and sat sprawling in a chair. Gil suspected he'd been in bed fairly recently, and his clothes hadn't seen a washing machine for a bit too long. "I took your American Literature class last spring and wanted to talk to you about my grade."

"What about it?" Gil almost sighed, remembering the student now. Frank Linio.

"Well, I got a D, but my grades were a lot higher than that. I think you made a mistake."

"You had all summer to get hold of me. I was available."

"I went with my parents to Sicily all summer."

"I've been there myself. It's lovely. Where were you?"

"Catania. We have family there."

"Lovely place. I've been to Taormina, not far away."

"Well, that's why I never got in touch with you," Frank explained.

"I remember that we rented a nice little place near the beach just outside of town," Gil continued, "not far from the elevated cable car that takes you up to the main part of the city, where the Greek amphitheater is. Funny, but I remember having internet and cell phone service. Do they have them in Catania?"

"Well, you made a mistake with my grade," Frank said, ignoring the question.

"Probably," Gil agreed. "As I recall it should have been an F."

"But I got all B's in all my papers," the young man insisted.

Gil took out his gradebook. Most professors used some sort of grading software now, but he still used the classic gradebook.

"You did get two B's in two response papers," he said while holding his finger on the line in the book. "You also received an F on your midterm, and a D on the final paper. Additionally, you were absent six times, and had a cell phone absence for three more, for a total of nine. On that alone, I could drop your grade to a failure, but I didn't."

Gil leaned back in his chair. "As I remember you sat in the second to the last row on my left, and for the most part were on your phone. I believe that I mentioned it a couple of times in class, and even sent you emails. And the reason I said you should have gotten an F in the course is that your final paper was incredibly vacuous and at times completely inaccurate; it seemed that you hadn't ever opened the books you were writing about. For instance, I think you wrote that Huckleberry Finn was infatuated with Becky Thatcher and got lost in a cave with Injun Joe." That wasn't the worst he'd ever seen. He remembered one student who tried to convince him in his final paper that Heathcliff had divorced his wife so he could marry Catherine. That student *did* get an F in the course.

"Well, he was. You said so in your lecture." Frank was defiant.

"I doubt that I said any such thing. In fact, it would be impossible," Gil said firmly. "You have two of Mark Twain's most popular characters confused because you obviously didn't read either book. Let me give you a word of advice: try to get off your phone long enough to actually pay attention in class, and spend some time reading the material. You might find school to suddenly be a lot easier, and your grades would be far less of a mystery to you." Gil closed the gradebook.

"I'm on academic probation now thanks to you," Frank said.

"No. I had nothing to do with it. You earned academic probation all by yourself. Think of it as a second chance," Gil replied. "My guess is that you have other low grades, too? I doubt that only one D would put you on probation."

"I already talked to the other teachers. They won't change my grades either, but those were all science and business classes. I thought you could be more flexible."

"Why?" Gil's voice went up a few decibels. "Because it's just a bullshit humanities course, therefore it doesn't really count?" Frank was smart enough to remain silent. Gil spoke again, saying, "You should take academic probation as a sign? Maybe? No one's picking on you, Richard and no one owes you a grade. If you want better grades, then work for them. You just need to work a little harder. Richard, no one owes you anything, especially me. You don't get a trophy just for showing up, understand?"

Frank blinked a couple of times and decided that discretion was more important than asking Professor Sykes who Richard was. He waited a moment before quietly leaving the office.

# Chapter 5

Christina dug her fingers into Gil's back, just below his neck, and started to loosen the tense muscles on his left side. Gil had made an appointment with her right after he had seen her at the grocery store, he was now having second thoughts. His neck had been hurting for a couple of days, but she was making it more painful. As if reading his mind, she said, "This will probably hurt like hell for now. But it will feel better soon." She worked his muscles some more. "How are your kids doing?"

"Did I tell you about them being in college? I usually don't miss an opportunity to brag about them."

"Yes, I forgot. And that nephew? I think Richard was his name?" Gil's shoulders tensed up pushing against her fingers. "Oh. I see. Guess we shouldn't talk about him, right?"

"It's okay. Just got a call about him, actually, the day I ran into you in the grocery store. Let's just say that he messed up again."

"Got it. You just relax, and let me do the work here," she said moving down his back with her fingers.

"Is your divorce final? I remember you talking about it at the party."

"Yes," she said. "I literally had just filed when we had that nice long talk, although I'd separated from him over a year before. I had a great attorney, and she moved things along pretty well. Not a lot of B.S." She paused while concentrating on Gil's lower back. "She got famous working on the Mali divorce. You know? The couple who own TrendInventions? She was Anne Mali's attorney, Zoe Peters."

"Didn't someone go to jail?"

"Actually, the attorney for Michael Mali, a guy named Cargill, got five years, and Michael himself was in some kind of trouble. They tried to bribe the judge. Borman? Burman? I think he went to jail, too. It wasn't the first time he took a bribe."

"Sounds like you got one hell of an attorney. She doesn't just win, but puts the other attorney in jail, and the judge just for good measure."

"She's good, but it just happened that they got caught. According to the papers, the FBI had been investigating them for about a year. The two guys weren't even subtle about the whole thing. It was obvious they were soliciting bribes, and the FBI had both of them nailed dead to rights.

"Arrogant people never are subtle," Gil said. "They seem to think that everyone around them is too stupid to figure out what they are doing, even when it's pretty obvious."

Christina worked some more on Gil's back, and he finally relaxed.

He thought back to the conversation he'd had with Christina at the holiday party. She'd mentioned that she'd gotten married and pregnant right out of high school. It was clear to him that she was very bright, and probably could have taken an advanced degree, but was making the most of her opportunities. Then he remembered Richard, who'd screwed up every chance he'd had, and his back stiffened.

"Are you okay, Professor Sykes?"

"Sorry, just had a bad thought."

"Problems with your nephew again?" She'd already read about it in the newspaper.

"Of course."

"Sorry." She worked harder on his lower back. "I know what it's like to have someone giving you problems in your life. Sometimes my ex-husband makes me angry. What bothers me the most is that he's spent the last eight years of his life partying—smoking pot and drinking. Whenever I talk to him, it's like having the same conversation over again, as if the drugs and alcohol have him permanently stuck at eighteen. I almost don't want my son to go with him for visitation. I worry that he's driving while stoned, or drunk, or both, and, of course, he's not a good influence. Not sure what to do."

"I understand. You might need to see an attorney and adjust his visitation, but most kids figure things out. You don't want to come off as the mean parent who kept him from his father, but you also need to keep him safe."

"Well, my ex-husband might just do it to himself. He missed the last few weekend visits. I was upset at first, but then realized that it might be for the best. It's just hard on our son.

"There," she said as she finished up the massage. "You should be ready for your trip now. You really should get one of those neck supporting pillows for the plane. Be sure to make an appointment with me when you get back."

***

Gil got off the plane in Chicago and went through the walkway to Midway Airport. His flight had been on time, and he'd been there several times before, so it was a quick walk to the luggage turntable and then out to get a cab for the fifteen-minute ride to the Palmer House. He remembered the first time he'd flown to Chicago. The flight from Albany to O'Hare had taken two hours, and the trip to his hotel had taken two and a half. He'd landed during rush-hour traffic. Ever since then, he'd flown to Midway.

The conference had already started. He had burnt out on academic conferences long ago and had only come as moral support for Valerie. A text from her lit up his phone as soon as he turned it on after landing.

R you in Chicago?

Yes. B at htl soon

K

His room was small, and it smelled of tobacco smoke. He remembered again why he hated going to conferences: a long weekend of shitty hotel rooms and bad food.

Valerie met him in the main foyer. She was standing next to a potted tree.

"Hiding behind the palm, I see," Gil said.

"Hi, Gil." She smiled. She was dressed in an oversized mustard-colored winter coat to fend off the Chicago climate. He remembered her propensity for wearing coats that made her short thin stature look even shorter and thinner, as if she were hiding behind the coat trying to disappear. He wondered if it was some sort of coping strategy.

"Hi, Val. Did you get the last batch of notes I sent in October?"

"Yes, and thanks. You're always a big help."

"Sorry I couldn't do more, but my life got a little hectic, again."

"I know. How are things going with your nephew?"

"As well as can be expected. He might not go to jail if he doesn't mess up for the next year or so, but the judge and the DA have had enough of him, and I don't blame them.

At Las Vegas the previous year, for the same annual conference, they'd presented together with one of her colleagues from Chamberlain. Marion had planned on going, but had a deadline pushed up, so he had gone alone, so he and Valerie had spent some time together at the hotel after they'd presented at a roundtable. Mostly they sat in the casino watching people dressed in their pajamas giving their money away to the mafia. They'd rented a car together and had taken a day trip to Hoover Dam the day after the conference ended. It had been warm and sunny, and they'd spent time walking along the huge dam and then up the staircase on the Arizona side, gazing out over Lake Mead. Then they toured the museum and ate at the snack bar before driving back to the hotel around sunset.

"Did you have a nice flight?"

"The plane landed, and I walked away."

"That bad?"

"No. I just hate to fly. I like arriving and am always grateful to the captain that he got me on the ground in one piece."

"I got here yesterday. You didn't miss much. Did Marion come along?"

"No," he said, "she's not interested unless the place is warm and she can soak up some sun near a pool." He grinned. "When are you scheduled?"

"Tomorrow afternoon."

"Good. So what do you want to do now?"

"I promised my friend that I'd go to her presentation on feminist reverberations in Proust's *Swann's Way*. You want to come along?"

"Sure."

They wandered around the conference rooms until they found the right one. People were still drifting in, and Gil and Valerie sat near the front. The presentation was attention-grabbing, but nothing Gil hadn't heard before. While Proust's sensibilities were ahead of his time, especially when it came to the psychology of women, and he had enormous writing talent, Gil always felt that scholars had a tendency to read a bit too much into the gay French dilettante and social climber. Afterward, they left and went to the Art Institute to look at some of the paintings, stopping for a long moment at the huge Seurat, *Sunday Afternoon on the Island of La Grande Jatte,* and then found a restaurant for dinner.

While Gil had read through her paper, had offered numerous suggestions and had even rewritten a few paragraphs, he was still not sure how Valerie had found the information. She'd been very quiet in the museum, and Gil had also been subdued. The business with Richard had left him drained. The public defender had started a long series of stall tactics to try to get some time between Richard's screw up and his sentencing. If he managed to stay out of trouble, the judge might be persuaded to go easier on him. Right now the judge was looking for a minimum of two years in prison.

Gil resolved that he wasn't ready to bend anyone's ear, especially Valerie's, with his problems. He sipped a bourbon and soda; she had an old fashioned. Valerie had appreciated the fact that he hadn't pressed for details. He had taken much of her research on faith and had simply helped her out with some of the literary history and some of the arguments she was making. After she finished half her drink, she sat back and took a deep breath. He could feel her relax for the first time since they'd met that morning in the hotel lobby. She looked at him and cleared her throat.

"You remember the earthquake in Haiti several years ago?"

"Yes," Gil said, "I read an article about how most of the aid money had been stolen by the Haitian government."

"That was no surprise," Valerie replied with a degree of certainty that implied more than theoretical knowledge.

"You've had experience?"

"Unfortunately, I've had quite a bit of experience with the Haitian government, especially their Ministry of Culture. When they don't have their hand out, they're busy being obstructionists just for the hell of it. Think of a country being run entirely by the stupid, spoiled, and idle rich, all of them related to each other."

"Oh, I can imagine one or two countries like that," Gil said, then took a long drink and looked around for the waitress.

"That's why it took me so long to get to where I can publish. It took over three years to locate the documents after they had been found." She took a breath. "Let me start at the beginning. The earthquake had flattened almost all of Port-au-Prince, as many of us saw on the news. But like most cities that are a few hundred years old, Port-au-Prince is built in layers. From before the time of Columbus, newer cities were built on top of old ones, and they created levels much like any of the old cities in Europe. If you go under the City of London, for instance, you will find layer after layer of ruins, including a Roman amphitheater far below.

"Port-au Prince was originally a native port, and then a Spanish outpost, eventually coming under the control of France. They ultimately exterminated or enslaved the native Amerindian populations, but then it went into a decline and became a port of call for buccaneers and other pirates. One in particular was known as Black Caesar, sometimes called Jean the Mulatto. He was an escaped slave from the Louisiana territory. This was before the American Revolution."

"You don't hear much about black pirates," Gil commented.

"There were a number of them, mostly escaped slaves," Valerie replied. "I hadn't heard much about them myself. History tends to ignore them in favor of the more notorious white Caribbean pirates like Blackbeard, Henry Morgan, or Anne Bonny and Mary Reid. The weird thing is that there was more than one black pirate captain, and at least one called Black Caesar, and they did very well as pirates go. They treated piracy like a business and avoided the showy stuff that got both Blackbeard and Morgan into trouble. The Black Caesar I found also had a democratic sensibility, maybe because he'd been a slave, and most of his crew was made up of escaped slaves. You can see how the culture of the times would avoid lionizing them as heroes, but instead latch on to the more bloodthirsty—and light-skinned—outlaws, to write about in the newspapers and novels of the time. There was probably little market for the disturbing image of well-armed and well-organized free black men on a pirate ship."

"I'd have to agree with that. Nothing more disturbing to a slave owner than a well-armed black man," Gil said.

Their dinners arrived, and, as they ate, Valerie continued her story.

"This particular Black Caesar, Jean the Mulatto, was smart enough to quit while he was ahead. After a few years, he gave the ship to his crew, under the command of Marcus Brady, his first mate, settled down in a stone mansion he had built in the hills above Port-au-Prince, and became a successful merchant, importing trade goods from Europe to the Caribbean. He used his skills as a pirate to train his captains on how to avoid falling prey to them: which areas of the Caribbean to avoid, which times of day were safest to sail. He even wrote a handbook for his captains to keep with them."

"Sounds resourceful," Gil remarked.

"He was some sort of genius, for sure," Valerie said. "Had he been white, he certainly wouldn't have been lost to history for hundreds of years.

"He died without any heirs, but his lifelong companion managed to run the business for another twenty years before he, too, passed away. The house was then confiscated by the government, which at that time was under French control. They used it for many years as a government building, and then abandoned it after the Haitian Revolution in the early eighteen hundreds."

"That's when the slaves actually took over the whole country; the revolution that President Jefferson refused to recognize."

"Right. And then France literally made them pay for it for the next hundred years to the tune of a hundred and fifty million francs," she said. "Now fast-forward to 2010 and the earthquake. While we usually think of earthquakes as burying people alive under tons of rubble, which they do, they also can open up huge cracks in the earth, which brings us to the article I just wrote.

"I had a student who went to Haiti after the earthquake, and while she was doing volunteer work with an NGO she came across the ruins of Jean's mansion. Part of a subbasement had been opened up by the earthquake. She found his diaries and papers, including the Charter of Agreement for his pirate crew and the Articles of Incorporation for his business. His importing business was one of the first employee-owned businesses. Each person had shares in the company, and each had a right to vote on policy, or propose changes to the company's rules or bylaws. He had kept careful records of their meetings, and kept the minutes, which is pretty amazing for the time, when most people, including most of his workers, were illiterate. He mentions in his diary of having the minutes read aloud and inviting any member to challenge or add to them."

"Wow," Gil said. "He's about two hundred years ahead of the curve. I don't think even the most liberal high-tech start-up is that democratic. It seems to me a lot of the founders of those high-tech businesses have degenerated into some sort of weird, simple-minded objectivism, like they're characters in an Ayn Rand novel."

"Yes. They do all really hate to pay taxes," Valerie said. "Anyway, while going through his papers, she came across these particular documents. I have a copy right here. And this is what took me three years to get out of the country. I think I met every relative of the current president, and perhaps the relatives of the last two going back to Papa Doc. Every one needed to be paid off, and I had to get a boatload of grant money to do it, but I have these copies with me, and the originals are in a safe place."

She pulled two papers out of her briefcase and handed them to Gil. They were written in French, but he knew enough to make a quick translation. She had highlighted certain phrases, many of which were common to both documents. The first essentially translated to "We hold these truths to be self-evident that all men are created equal;" the next phrase was basically, "Nature's God has given each of us the right to life liberty and pursuit of his own goals," and "We form this more perfect union in order to promote the general welfare of its members."

"Yes, I think you've got something here," Gil said. "But where does the Jefferson tie-in come along?"

"That is difficult to prove, and you need some imagination. Even though these phrases are similar to the Declaration of Independence and the Constitution, there's a remote chance that Jefferson simply stumbled across these constructions on his own. Either way, Jean's former crew ran out of luck."

"They attacked one ship too many?"

"Yes, indeed. An American colonial frigate in disguise that had been well-armed. They conquered the pirates and took them to Richmond, where all of the black sailors were sold into slavery, with one in particular, the ship's captain, Marcus Brady, ...."

"Going to Tuckahoe Plantation," Gil exclaimed.

"Exactly." Valerie said. "Since he was captain, it was his duty to carry the Charter. He kept it as part of his legacy, and passed it on to his daughter, whom he taught to read and write in French and English. According to the few references I could find about her, she was very pretty, incredibly smart, and would eventually catch the attention of the young Jefferson.

"So there's the connection. She obviously must have shared her father's papers with her lover—this was years before Sally Hemings, and years before the Declaration of Independence or the Constitution. Jefferson's cousin sold the girl after he'd found out that young Thomas was having an affair with her. She ended up being a nanny to the master's children of a large plantation in southern Virginia."

"Wow." Gil sipped his drink before saying, "I can imagine how this'll go over. Not just a black man, but a pirate to boot. You can't make this stuff up." He hesitated for only a second before saying, "You can prove this?"

"Pretty much all of it. The girl, who was about fourteen, was sold around the time Jefferson would have been sixteen. That's part of the record of sales, so we need to interpret events a little. There's no smoking gun, but there's plenty of evidence pointing in the right direction. What would be absolutely conclusive would be to find a copy of the pirate Charter of Agreement in the original French in the hand of Jean in Jefferson's papers, but my guess is that they're long gone."

"Had I been Jefferson, I would have burnt them and scattered the ashes," Gil said.

"Perhaps, but he was probably arrogant enough to think he'd made it up on his own, conveniently forgetting about the Charter. I doubt he'd have destroyed it. After all, to his credit, he did preserve and donate thousands of volumes to various libraries. It wouldn't have been like him to actually destroy a document."

"Intriguing thought," Gil said. "Who'd have the papers now if he'd kept them?"

"That's another story," Valerie said. "He could have left them with his papers at the Library of Congress, or in Monticello, the University of Virginia, which he founded, William and Mary College, his alma mater, or someplace else. He even spent five years in Paris just before the French Revolution. It's impossible to say. Some of his papers could have been destroyed when the British sacked Washington in the War of 1812. This was long before the custom of creating monuments to your ego known as presidential libraries caught on."

"My guess is that what you have is all you're going to get. And it's amazing you have that much."

"I agree," Valerie said, and finished her drink. They paid their bill and walked back to the hotel. The breeze off Lake Michigan chilled them both, and the shattering noise from the passing EL train kept them silent. Neither of them wanted to turn in for the night, so they went to the small bar behind the reception desk for a nightcap. It was as if the cold evening and the noise from the EL had quashed their desire to talk. She finished her drink first. He followed her to the elevator and together they rode up to her floor. He walked her to her room, and then went to his room. It still reeked of cigarettes.

# Chapter 6

Jean was working in the office of his warehouse when his assistant Carlo brought the sad news. The *Rouge Noir* had been sunk by a Colonial frigate from Virginia. The frigate had opened up with an unexpected broadside as the *Rogue* pulled alongside to board, and the ship went down in mere minutes. Most of the crew had drowned, but a few had been rescued, and then taken to Richmond to be sold as slaves. One of the ship's cabin boys had escaped, tucked into a floating barrel that drifted away with the other wreckage of the boat, and hiding himself from the crew of the American ship. He drifted for several days before being picked up by a French merchant on the way to Haiti, and he was the one who told the story of how it had been a trap: the frigate's cannons had been hidden under tarps, and the ship had been a decoy, made to look like an unarmed merchant.

Jean sat down, and his eyes rolled back in his head when he heard the news. Carlo grabbed him to keep him from falling off the chair, and then got him some water mixed with rum.

"Did the cabin boy say anything about Marcus?" Jean asked.

"Nothing about any particular member of the crew, but you know Marcus. If anyone lived, he did." Carlo affectionately patted Jean's hand. While Carlo had never met Marcus, Jean had entertained him with stories of their adventures. Jean and Carlo had met soon after Jean had left the *Rouge Noir* and decided to start an importing-exporting business in Haiti.

To that day, Jean still smiled when he thought about how they'd met. Carlo was working the shell game near the docks, a deceptively simple game where he would place a dried pea under one of three large oyster shells, and then move them around. The "mark," usually a sailor who had a pocketful of money after getting paid for a voyage, would guess where the pea was, and get it right a few times. Then his "luck" would change, and, no matter how hard he tried, he would never be able to guess where the pea was. Carlo expertly encouraged his victim until he was out of money.

Jean watched, amused, and noted the moments when the young man scooped up the pea with the long fingernail on his middle finger and tucked it into his palm. For good measure, after his mark guessed wrongly for the third or fourth time and was getting suspicious and angry, Carlo would deposit the pea under another shell, and turn it over to show the man where it "really" was. Jean watched, and Carlo noticed him watching, observed his finely tailored clothes, and took him for a wealthy merchant, but too smart for the shell game.

After his mark ran out of money, Carlo took his shells and the pea and put them away. Some of the men waiting around were disappointed, because they'd wanted to try their luck, but Carlo had a potentially much larger score in his sights.

"Are you new to Port-au-Prince?" he asked Jean, smiling, his light brown eyes wide, while sizing him up.

"Yes and no. I've been here before, but not to stay."

"You will be staying here then?"

"I'm thinking about it."

"Then I must show you around," Carlo insisted.

Jean was attracted to the beautiful, smart young man who was obviously living by his wits, and Carlo had been equally attracted to Jean, but for other reasons. Carlo tried to find out which hotel the obviously wealthy man was staying in with the idea of breaking into his room. When they began to run out of places for Carlo to take his new friend, Jean suggested they go find some place to eat since it was already past mid-day, and breakfast for him had been soon after sunrise.

Carlo decided to take whatever he could get. "I know of a great tavern not far from here. They have the best rum, and they always have stew on the boil, and so we could eat and drink. He pulled out a wad of money that had recently belonged to a few hapless sailors. "And it will be my treat for my new friend."

"No," Jean said. "I insist that I pay. Lead on."

Carlo led Jean through a winding series of streets in a less populated rundown section of town, certainly an unusual place for a popular tavern. They ended on a remote dead-end street.

"I must have taken a wrong turn," Carlo said, and moved to step behind Jean as if he was walking back down the street to get his bearings. He quickly picked up a piece of wood and turned to threaten Jean and steal his money only to find his intended victim pointing a cocked and loaded pistol right at his heart.

They often joked that their relationship had gotten off to a rough start.

Carlo had looked hard and long at the pistol pointed at his heart, dropped the club on the ground and burst out laughing. Jean was taken aback for a moment, but then he started to laugh, too, never taking the gun off Carlo.

He then marched his larcenous new acquaintance to a tavern and bought him something to eat. Trust, friendship, and eventually love came later.

Jean was still trying to comprehend the news about Marcus. "But now he's a slave? Again? He must be distraught." Jean sipped some more rum. "I told him to be careful. Those Americans are tricky. They're worse than the British." He looked into the warehouse stacked with kegs of rum, dried ginger, vanilla beans, sugar, molasses, and bales of cotton, anything that came from the Caribbean. Jean had become a very wealthy man, and Carlo his business manager.

Jean had taken his share of many raids that he had saved up and left the *Rogue Noir* with Marcus as the captain five years earlier, but he'd strongly encouraged them to not keep to privateering for much longer. The odds were against them, and the political climate was changing in Europe. He figured that France would seek peace with England sooner than later, and the French privateers would be left without a protector. The crew, however, wanted to keep on, and Jean didn't blame them. They'd all made a lot of money, and it was unlikely they'd ever be able to make that kind of money in any other business, even as free black men.

He opened his desk, and took out a rolled up vellum document, tied with a green ribbon. It was the original Charter. He'd made a copy of it and had given it to Marcus, whom he had taught how to read and write. Jean gazed at the calfskin document, written in his careful and precise hand in India ink, reading the same words over and over, but not really reading them. Carlo asked him if he wanted more to drink, but Jean didn't hear him. He just continued to stare at the Charter, thinking about Marcus and all of his friends on board the *Rogue* now dead, or worse.

***

*1700s, Colonial Virginia*

Marcus was on the auction block at the market in downtown Richmond. His size assured his captors that they would get a good price, but some slave owners were afraid to bid on him because they could see he was not one who would tame easily. They didn't want a slave who might cause trouble or intimidate their drivers. So while he fetched a good price, it wasn't what his captors had expected. Marcus and the other two field slaves recently bought at the auction had their hands bound together and the rope was then tied to the back of a wagon loaded with supplies from the stores in Richmond. They walked along behind the slow-moving, heavily loaded wagon as they were all taken to their new home. Occasionally, they had to pull over to the side of the road, being careful not to step in the wet, buggy ditch to let a rider on horseback come through, but the tedium of the long walk made Marcus slip into deep reverie, and he was quiet, still in shock over the loss of his ship—and deeply ashamed.

He should have seen it coming, he mused, and played that day over and over in his head. It had started with a bad feeling about the ship they'd attacked; it was too easy. The ship hadn't even tried to outrun them, just struck their sails as soon as the *Rogue Noir* began pursuit. He'd tried to convince the men to let it go, but they'd insisted. One more ship and then return to port, they'd said. They hadn't even manned the cannons when they'd pulled up abreast of the frigate, not that it would have made much difference. The next thing he saw was a bright flash followed by tremendous explosions as the cannonballs ripped into the side of his ship and their own powder magazine exploded. He was knocked out, but came to in the water, knocked clear of the sinking ship. It looked like all but a handful of his crew had drowned.

*Typical of the Americans to overdo it. And now there is no cargo for them to capture because it went down with the Rogue Noir.* Had he planned such an attack, he would have aimed the cannons higher, destroying the sails and the upper decks, making sure not to set off the powder magazine, and then his men would have boarded the ship and looted it. *And* he would have left the survivors on a floating ship where someone could find them. But now, the only way the Americans could get any money, other than the bounty on sinking a pirate ship, was to sell the men they'd fished out of the water, including Marcus who was at that point wondering if perhaps the rest of the crew, those who had drowned, had gotten the better deal.

After walking most of the day, the slaves arrived at their new home. Marcus thought that it looked to be a well-run and maintained plantation as he saw the gently sloping hills, orchards, paddocks, and well-kept gardens. It was far more pleasant looking than the salt works in Cannel Island, but he knew that he would be a slave again, probably for the rest of his life.

He could barely feel his legs as they untied his hands and he walked slowly to the small cabin that would be his home. His driver left him after telling him that he would be working in the fields starting at sunrise the next day.

Marcus could feel the copy of the Charter under his shirt, the copy that Jean had given him. When he was alone in the cabin, he took it out of the leather case and unrolled it. The Charter had not gotten very wet from his short time in the sea. He had put it in his coat just before they sighted the American ship; it had been his intention to propose that they invoke the disbanding clause after they returned to port, and had been rereading it to make sure they did it right.

If the men had voted on disbanding, as he'd hoped, the cargo and all the money held in common for the operation of the vessel would have been distributed according to the shares owned by each crew member, and the ship would be offered for sale to those who might want to continue to sail her. If none bid on her, she would have been sold outright and the money from the sale evenly divided among the crew. Now there was no ship, nor cargo, nor crew.

Marcus immediately found a place to hide the document. He put the vellum scroll back in its leather pouch, tying the straps, put it in the gunny sack, and secreted it in a space between the walls, working it through a small knothole.

Then Marcus sat down on the corner of his bed and cried.

# Chapter 7

The room was dead silent. While a good portion of the attendees were at least intrigued and possibly pleased with Val's ideas, a large minority was not. Some people fidgeted, and others looked around the room staring at the tacky ornamentation, fit more for a wedding reception than a conference.

Valerie asked for questions. There was a pause, and one person raised his hand.

"Ms. Dymond," he said, "are you familiar with the latest historical scholarship on Thomas Jefferson?"

"Some of it, yes" Valerie responded. "And feel free to call me Professor or Doctor Dymond."

"Sure, Professor," the man said, turning a little pink. "My point is that this is the first I've heard of any of this. Wouldn't you think that the historians of this time period would have found this out a long time ago?"

"Why?" Valerie asked him, not to be contentious, but genuinely curious.

"That's what they do for a living," he said.

"Yes, but this is what *I* do for a living, and I'm just presenting what I've found."

"So you have the document?"

"Yes. A full-sized high definition scan. The original is in the government archives in Haiti."

"I mean," he said, nursing a dramatic pause a little too long, "the one that was in Jefferson's papers."

"That I don't have," Valerie said.

"She admitted that at the start of the talk," Gil mentioned, helping her out. "Did you arrive late?"

"Like Gil said, you need to use a little imagination." Valerie took over the conversation. "And I have thoroughly documented the piece and have traced what history of Jean the Mulatto that I can. I've also done an analysis of the language of the time, the French commonly spoken in the Louisiana territory, and in Haiti, and came to my conclusions." She gave him a nod. "You are free to disagree, of course."

"My scholarship is not based on imagination," he declared.

"Then it must be very boring," Gil said under his breath.

Valerie smiled, and asked for more questions from the audience.

Some of the comments were favorable, but others were not and those who disagreed seemed to be getting ruder and louder by turn. Some were blurting out what was on their minds regardless of the rules of order: "This is irresponsible scholarship at best." "Political correctness, that's all it is."

Valerie tried to explain that she'd done many years of research to validate her point, and that hers was not a hasty claim made for maximum effect, but her words fell on the deaf ears of those who were not happy with the idea that a black man might have penned the most famous words of the Declaration of Independence many years before Jefferson.

Gil and Valerie took the side exit into a long hallway, and then left the conference center through a door into the parking garage. Once outside, they found a small corner coffee shop, and ducked in and found seats.

"So that went over really well," Valerie said.

"I'd say about half of them would have given you a standing ovation, and certainly agreed with you."

"I'd say the other half would do something else entirely. Have they had a lynching in this state recently?" She asked.

"Not this far north, not as a rule," Gil said. They both laughed. "When you roast someone's sacred cow, they don't take it lightly."

After coffee, they returned to the conference hotel and went together to a few presentations. Valerie did not stray far from her friend, and Gil understood. The hostility from some people they passed was palpable. However, the editor of a prestigious academic journal sought her out, spoke with her at length, and then gave her a business card. She asked Valerie to be sure to send the manuscript of her presentation to her journal when it was ready. That lifted Val's sprits, and Gil felt glad for her, too. Once published, the criticism would be confined to what people could reasonably argue and prove, although they both knew that was almost as cutthroat as what had happened in the lecture room.

A famous academic was giving a lecture late that afternoon as the keynote address, so the buzz around Val's presentation died down as everyone geared up to hear what he had to say about the state of humanities and higher education in general, which was not very heartening.

Gil actually had met the speaker years back when he was still in graduate school. The guy had come to his campus for a semester as a guest lecturer. Gil and the other students were in awe of him for a while, but it wore off for Gil when he realized that the guy essentially liked to hear the sound of his own ideas, and if he liked one of your ideas, he was more than happy to make it his own. Needless to say, Gil wasn't interested in attending the lecture, and Valerie wasn't interested in being confronted by either a newfound fan or someone—more often than not a man—who felt the need to "set her straight," usually by giving her information she already knew or citing a scholar she'd already read or whose work she was familiar with.

She idly wondered if a white male would even attempt to do that to another white male; certainly it seemed a few had no problem doing so to a woman of color.

After seeing a late showing of a discounted movie that had worn out its welcome in the major cinemas, they came back late to the hotel and were both relieved to see that few people from the conference were around. Gil wasn't tired, so a drink in the hotel bar was their next order of business. They talked of anything other than the presentation, and then Gil walked Valerie to her room, where she kissed him on the cheek.

"Thank you for rescuing me." She smiled.

"It's what I do." Gil smiled back.

***

Gil fell asleep quickly and overslept. He'd shut off his phone before the presentation and forgot to turn it back on, so the alarm didn't go off. Suddenly remembering that he had a flight to catch, he looked at the clock on the nightstand and jumped out of bed. Gil made it to the airport, breezed through security, and was the last one on the plane. A flight attendant guided him to his seat, said, "Welcome aboard, Dr. Sykes. We were hoping you'd make it." The plane lifted off as he buckled up.

When they landed, there was a light snow on the ground. Gil took the shuttle bus to his car and drove the hour and a half home. The door was locked, and Marion's car was gone. He went into the house and turned up the thermostat because he felt cold. There was a note on the table from Marion saying to call her. He took out his phone, switched it back on, and listened as it chimed at least a dozen times.

***

Richard was drinking Friday night at a bar noted for cheap but strong drinks. He knew his mom was home asleep, deeply exhausted. She'd been putting in ten-hour days. Of course, since she was management, there was no overtime pay. Richard knew there was no chance of her actually waking up before he got home.

"I want another rum and Coke," he shouted across the bar.

"Maybe you should think about it?" The bartender, a short man with a weary look, said. "That's your fifth drink, and it looks to me like you had a few before you got here."

"You cutting me off, you asshole?" Richard drunk was Richard belligerent.

"I am now," the bartender said, and nodded to the door. "I can call you a cab."

"You think I'm a fucking pussy?"

"No. You just had a little too much to drink. I'll call a cab for you." The man took out his cell phone and started to punch in a number. Richard reached across the bar and tried to slap it out of his hand, but the man was too fast for him. He pulled back, and Richard's arm went through empty space until it slammed into the side of a beer tap.

"Ow! You fucking hit me, you asshole."

"No, buddy, you hit yourself. Why don't you settle down and wait for the cab?"

"Fuck you," Richard screamed, and broke his glass against the bar, then pointing the sharp end at the bartender, who reached under the bar, took out a short baseball bat, and knocked the glass out of Richard's hand in one quick motion. Richard's hand was cut from the broken glass.

"What? Did you see that in a fucking cowboy movie, you jerk? It doesn't work that way in real life. Get the fuck out of my bar, you son of a bitch," the bartender said as he came around the end of the bar with the bat raised. Richard ran for the door, managing to knock over a table that had some glasses and an empty beer pitcher on it on his way. They smashed to the floor. He looked behind him and smiled, raising his bloody hand in the air, middle finger extended. The bartender chased him out to the parking lot. Richard got in his mother's car and drove with the gas pedal floored. He was doing at least twice the speed limit before he even got to the road, almost hitting a taxicab as it was turning into the parking lot.

He was sucking the cut on his hand. It was deep enough to need stitches, but he knew not go to the emergency room. Richard decided he'd take the highway home and wake his mom; she could drive him to the hospital so he wouldn't get into any trouble. He was already working on a story that she'd believe, but while nursing his hand, he passed the on-ramp to the highway, and took the next right, which was the off-ramp, not noticing the stop signs and the bright red sign that told him to turn back. Richard was doing just a hair over eighty going the wrong way in what was the slower lane of the highway. A car came at him head on, but swerved into the passing lane, the driver blasting his horn and flashing his lights. Richard turned to give him the one finger salute and didn't see the semi directly in front of him.

Tad had been driving truck for thirty years. He liked driving at night because there was less traffic, and he didn't mind sleeping during the day. His rig was bound for Albany with a load of snow tires, and he wondered if he should stop for coffee, since he was a bit ahead of schedule, and didn't want to get there and have to wait for the warehouse to open at five a.m. The sign before the exit promised a 24/7 diner, but he wasn't sure if it was the one he'd stopped at before on this run, the diner that had a convenient parking lot for trucks. He turned his head to read the name on the second sign for the exit a mile before the ramp. He'd have to start slowing down if he wanted to get off the highway in a mile. The sound of a blasting horn brought his eyes front, and he saw the car in front him quickly swerve into the left-hand lane. Then he saw Richard's car a fraction of a second before it hit the front of his truck head on. He slammed on the brakes and the rig jackknifed, coming up off the ground on the left side. He fought the wheel back left and then right to keep the cab in front of the trailer. For a moment it looked like he'd lose control, his truck would go over, but the rig came back down on the dirty side, and the clean side stayed up. It came to a stop in the middle of the highway, blocking all four lanes. The driver's door was jammed, so Tad crawled out of the window and jumped down from the truck.

What was left of Richard's car was a hundred yards up the road in two pieces. He ran to the car, but he might as well have walked. Tad took out his phone and called 911. He then set flares on both sides of the road and started flagging cars down with his flashlight.

The state police called Marion in the middle of the night because Claudia had been incoherent. Marion called Gil, but his phone wasn't on.

He called her back as soon as he got her messages. She answered on the second ring.

"Sorry, Marion, I shut off my phone yesterday and forgot to turn it back on. Just got in the door."

"That's okay. It's not like you could do anything anyway." Her voice hitched a little as she said, "There's nothing anyone can do. He died on impact. They need to know which funeral home Claudia wants him to go to after the coroner finishes up. The driver of the truck is okay, though. His truck cut the top of the car off. I actually feel sorry for him. His truck is a total loss."

"That's good," Gil said, "I guess. He didn't hurt anyone. Right?" He had no idea what to say; his words were all coming out wrong. Marion was silent at the other end of the phone. "Do you want me to come over?" Gil finally asked

"I was just getting ready to leave," she said. "A doctor gave Claudia a shot of something. She was out of her mind, but she's out cold now. I took her home and put her to bed."

"Okay. I'll see you when you get home. We can call the kids later."

"That makes sense. No need to upset them before we have to," she said.

He said goodbye, but she'd already hung up the phone. He unpacked his clothes and took a shower. She came in as he was dressing in fresh clothes. It was Saturday so he wouldn't have to worry about reading or grading papers or getting ready for work. Marion looked very tired but mostly strained, totally defeated. She went into her bathroom to clean up. Gil put a frying pan on the stove to make eggs; he hadn't eaten since late afternoon the day before.

"Are you hungry?" he yelled in the direction of the bathroom.

"Yes," she shouted through the door.

"I'll make you some eggs."

"Thanks."

He set out two plates, and made breakfast, even though it was midafternoon. She came out of the bathroom, her hair in a towel. Her eyes were very red, but she looked a little less distraught than when she had first gotten home, although she remained quiet. They ate in silence.

"Poor Claudia," Gil finally said. "This might break her. I can't see how she'll survive it."

"I know."

"That stupid, stupid shit," Gil said, and finished his breakfast without another word. Marion picked at her food, managing to eat only a little.

She finally told Gil about meeting the police at the hospital emergency room. They'd found her cell number in Claudia's phone. Claudia had been so incoherent that the staff had no idea what to do, so they took a chance and called. The evening watch commander had been cordial and professional, and the hospital staff was sympathetic, to Claudia especially, but she'd sensed a strong undercurrent of blame.

There was no ambiguity here about a car "accident;" they all referred to it as a collision, even the truck driver who met briefly with Marion and Claudia after he was discharged. He was gentlemanly and told Claudia he was deeply sorry. But it was obvious to Gil that, had Richard survived, he would have gone to jail for a long time. It hadn't been an accident; it was a collision that was entirely his fault.

Grief and anger alternated as Marion and Gil tried to relax. Gil sought refuge in television, but the station had been left on a movie channel, and the scene playing was in the middle of a car chase from a movie that was mostly car chase scenes separated by small doses of plot. Gil quickly turned to a cooking show, where someone was preparing a shrimp dish with an astonishing amount of butter. He picked up the Saturday paper, but read the same lead paragraph on the main story above the fold a half dozen times before putting it back on the coffee table. Marion was in the reclining chair with her e-book, but quickly fell asleep.

Gil was restless, even though he had gotten little sleep the night before, so he went for a walk. The November air was chill and damp, so he adjusted his route accordingly, shortening it by about half a mile. He wanted to walk until he could no longer think, but no matter what, something would pop into his head. Eventually, he managed to just walk and breathe in the biting air, pushing everything out of his head. When he got back to the house, he was in a neutral mood. His face was red, and he felt warm and flushed. The heating system was kicking in, and dry warm air streamed at him from the duct near the front door. He saw that Marion had moved from the chair, and the bedroom door was closed. He peeked in, just cracking the door open. He could see her sleeping, breathing gently, neatly tucked in on her side of the bed. Even when she slept alone, Marion stayed on her half. Gil made a cup of coffee and turned on the TV with the sound very low. He sipped while watching an old movie, one that he'd seen before about a bunch of people in a house on an island in Florida waiting for a storm to come. Edward G. Robinson was taking a bath and smoking a cigar.

Gil fell asleep long before the storm.

# Chapter 8

Gil's words proved to be prophetic. Claudia imploded, and had to be almost carried from place to place by her sister, or some other friend or relative in waiting. He and Marion made all the arrangements for the funeral, from meeting with the funeral director to ordering the flowers. Of course, the casket had to be closed, but Gil found a photo of Richard in a frame on the shelf against the paneled wall in the den. It had been taken in a studio when he was a teenager. Gil had cleaned up the dust from the frame and brought it to the funeral home.

The director, a small, thin man with an air that reminded Gil of a bird of prey, a very old bird of prey, was waiting for him.

"I want to talk to you for a minute," he said, and then went on without a waiting for a reply. "There is a matter concerning the order that you placed." He went over the long, itemized list; Gil and Marion had sat with Claudia and the director a few days before, but Gil had made almost all of the decisions. He'd decided there was no need for embalming, even though the funeral director had pushed hard for it. Gil tried to be as delicate as he could around Claudia, but he'd seen the remains; they had given him nightmares for the last three nights. And there was no need for what the director had euphemistically referred to as "restoration." The casket would be shut tight for the whole service.

But there was the wake, the coffin, the vault, and the funeral procession to the cemetery where Gil and Marion had quickly bought a plot not far from Richard's father. The director had also placed the obituary, which Gil had written, so there was a charge for that, too.

The man was insistent, so Gil gave him his credit card, musing that he'd probably done a credit check on Claudia and panicked. Gil could understand that it was doubtless very hard for the man to collect anything once the services were over, especially if there were problems with an estate that took a long time to settle in probate, or simply having to deal with someone who had very little money, like Claudia, but it didn't look as if the man or his business were doing poorly when it came to finances. Gil had the morbid thought while handing him the credit card that of all people, a funeral director would understand that there was no way to take it with you.

After settling the bill, Gil went back home. It was a few days before Thanksgiving break, and his two kids had come home early. Gil's students got an extra-long holiday, as well.

It felt odd to Gil and Marion to have a full house again: going to the fridge to find leftovers already gone, turning on the TV to a strange station, wet towels in the bathroom, shoes by the door, and other signs of life. Gil had actually seen very little of his children during the course of the funeral preparations. He knew that, while they were there to go to their cousin's funeral, they also were catching up with friends.

Mary was in the kitchen on the phone when Gil got back from the funeral home. She looked up and smiled at him, and he smiled back. "Your Mom?" he mouthed. She nodded. Gil used a combination of sign language and speaking without sound. "Let me talk when you're done." Mary nodded and answered her mother's question.

Gil went into the living room. The weekend paper was still on the folding tray table beside his chair. He hadn't had much of a chance to sit and read, so he picked it up.

It wasn't long before Mary came in with her phone.

"Here, Dad," she said, handing it to him.

"Is she with Aunt Claudia?" Gil asked.

"What do you think?" Mary was exasperated. She had never been a big fan of her aunt or her cousin.

"Hi. How's it going?"

"Not great."

"Looks like Mary's getting some dinner ready," Gil said looking in the kitchen.

"You guys eat without me," Marion replied. "I might have to watch her tonight.

"For Pete's sake, Marion. She's a grown woman."

"Sorry," she said. There was a long pause. "I just worry that she might do something."

"Other than play her usual head games?"

"Gil, please. Her boy's dead."

"Yes. But it wasn't like he had nothing to do with it. Unexpected but not unanticipated."

"Don't be so mean."

"I'm just being honest. By the way, I settled up with the funeral home today. Everything's taken care of. The flowers will be there tomorrow morning, and the wake starts at noon, like we planned."

"Good. I'm glad it's taken care of."

"That funeral director didn't give me a lot of choice. I thought he might repossess Richard's body there for a minute."

Another long pause as his attempt to lighten her mood failed.

"I'll be by tomorrow morning to change my clothes."

"Okay. I'll make sure the kids are ready. Jason might need a new jacket. All he has is the one from his high school graduation and it was snug on him then, and besides, it's a light tan.

"Have him try it on tonight. You can go out tomorrow morning if he needs one; get navy blue, not black, and give him one of your white dress shirts and a pair of shoes. I think all he owns are sneakers and flip flops."

"I wouldn't be surprised. He does go for the gutter-punk look. But his teeth are far too straight and nice to pull it off."

"Yes, the orthodontics did pay off. He's very handsome," Marion said. "I'll call you in the morning. Bye."

Gil went to the kitchen, where he placed the phone on the counter. "Don't make too much food. Your mom's staying at your aunt's house, and I have no idea where Jason is."

"I sort of planned on that." Mary said, and pointed to two plates of salad, and two hamburgers in the frying pan. "I heard you say Jason needs a new jacket. He's probably not far if you need to call him."

"Later," Gil said. "If I remember right, he'll be here when he gets hungry. He never was one for missing a meal." Gil looked at his daughter. "You, on the other hand, seem to be disappearing."

"I'm fine. School's been difficult this year. I have the internship plus a full load of classes, along with practice and track meets," Mary paused. "And not to sound too jaded, but good old Richard couldn't have picked a worse time, not that there is ever a good time, to kill himself."

"You think he did it on purpose?"

"Not consciously, maybe." Mary was thoughtful. "But he always was up for anything dangerous and stupid. It didn't take much. Like he constantly had to prove something. Or maybe he just had a death wish."

"That's true," Gil said. "So he got what he wanted maybe?"

"You, Mom, and Aunt Claudia have no idea. Just driving around town with him could be a terrifying experience," Mary said while she took the hamburgers out of the frying pan. "Well, maybe you have an idea, but Mom and Aunt Claudia are clueless." She added potato chips to the plates. "You want your burger on two slices of bread or open faced?"

"No bread, please. Your mom might be a little wiser than you think," Gil said, putting ketchup on his burger. "You're right about your Aunt Claudia, though."

Jason arrived just as they finished eating. He made himself a hamburger and put it on to cook. "Wow, real hamburger," he said. "The burgers they have at school are horrible."

"They can't be that bad," Gil said.

"They're chewy," Jason said. "Now, if the meat is all ground up, what is it that makes it chewy?"

"You don't wanna know?" Gil said.

"Right, Dad. You got it." Jason had made a very large hamburger out of all that was left of the meat and took the bowl of salad and the open bag of chips with him to the table.

Gil sat down across from him, still nibbling on his chips.

"Did you skip lunch?"

"No. I ate at Cathy's house."

Gil recalled that Cathy was his on-again-off-again-girlfriend-sometimes-with-benefits.

"How is she?"

"Fine. She might come to the wake tomorrow, but she has to work and still has classes. She's at Bradbury."

"Right. I see her on campus sometimes," Gil said. It had been eerie seeing his son's childhood friend on campus—the pretty brunette who used to eat ice pops in his kitchen and had been a regular at their dinner table for years. The first time she greeted him, he'd felt as if he were in the wrong place, as if he was supposed to be home, or at the community pool, not at work. A deep shift had happened in his life, and he hadn't really seen it until then. He knew that Richard's death, too, would also mark a deep change. He grasped it with his head, but not fully, not yet. "Your mom wants you to try on the jacket you wore for graduation. If it doesn't fit, we need to buy you a new one, tonight."

"Oh, Dad. I've got plans."

"They can wait. You came home early because of your cousin's funeral, remember? You'll have time to go out with your friends after tomorrow. Plus, you need to keep up with schoolwork. Exams are right after break. You're not used to a college schedule yet. It's not high school."

"Okay," Jason said. "Sorry. How is Aunt Claudia?"

"Pretty bad; your mom's staying with her tonight."

"Probably a good idea." He made short work of the hamburger and finished the bag of chips and the rest of the salad his sister had made. He was eating an ice pop when they went to the mall to buy a jacket.

*** 

The funeral parlor had the expected heavy floral aroma, some of which came from the actual flowers in the room, but most from hidden aerosol sprayers. The smell gave Gil an instant pounding headache. The family had turned out in force, which was a little unexpected since Richard had probably borrowed money, stolen from, or otherwise screwed over almost all of his friends and relatives. Gil supposed that sometimes the funeral really is for the living.

At one point, a very long-haired skinny man dressed in ratty jeans and a moth-eaten tie-dyed shirt walked in and went right up to the casket, obliviously cutting in front of the line. Gil moved to intercept him by extending his hand to shake. The skinny man roughly brushed it. He mumbled incoherently for a few minutes about losing his "bro, the best man alive," and then walked toward the door. Jason moved to intercept him, and Gil rushed up and put his hand on his son's shoulder, shaking his head.

Along with two members of the funeral home staff, Jason and Gil followed the man out, making sure he left the funeral home. Gil went back to the viewing and asked around. No one in the room seemed to know who he was.

Marion walked over to him. "Who was that?"

"Saint Peter?" Gil said. "Apparently, there's some sort of negotiation going on right as we speak." Marion looked at him, unamused. "Sorry," he said. "No one seems to know who he was. Perhaps we don't want to know?"

A new group of people arrived; Gil greeted them and spoke quietly. He and Marion had become the de facto reception line. Presently the minister from Claudia's church showed up and the service began. The minister was diplomatic as he lamented the tragic passing of such a young person, and praised Richard for his "spirited attitude," and "energetic soul," but obviously knew him well enough to not lay it on too thick.

After the service at the gravesite, many of the people went to Gil and Marion's for something to eat. Mary and Jason managed to change clothes and slip out of the house without much fanfare, and after a few hours all of the mourners, including Claudia, went home. Marion had offered to go with her, and Gil had bristled. After a cousin volunteered to drive Claudia home and keep an eye on her, Marion relented.

They were alone for the first time in over a week. They had used paper plates and disposable cups, and the caterer had put everything in foil trays, so there was no real cleanup. Everything went into garbage bags, which was environmentally inappropriate, but too convenient to resist. Gil took off his tie and jacket and sat in the armchair in the living room. He had set a plate of food aside and was munching on some appetizers while Marion finished wiping down the kitchen counters and putting leftovers in the fridge, which was already overloaded with food to be prepared for Thanksgiving dinner. She was banging things around and there where dangerous sounding noises coming from inside the old fridge when she finally slammed the door shut and came into the room.

"I'm angry with him," Marion announced.

"Who?"

"Richard, of course. He's managed to ruin Thanksgiving from now on for poor Claudia, and for us, too."

"Not forever."

"No. But for a while at least."

"Mary thinks he did it on purpose, at least subconsciously."

"She's a psychology major. She thinks everyone does everything on purpose, without knowing it." Marion sat on the couch and put her feet on the coffee table. "She'll be graduating this year."

"Yes. I was going to talk to her about graduate school, but she seems to be a little stressed."

"She's got a list of places she wants to apply to."

"Good. Maybe I'll sit and chat with her before she goes back. She has to go back and then come right back after exams. Too bad she couldn't get her professors to give her exams online."

"They can't. She has too many labs. Might be a good idea to mention graduate school, but go easy with her. She's just broken up with her boyfriend," Marion said as she massaged her feet. "They're both graduating, and neither of them is interested in marriage, or in moving in together. They could end up at opposite ends of the country with graduate school and all. It was her idea, but he's not taking it too well. She needs to finish moving out of his apartment. It's good her friends let her move in with them; she'd spent so much time there she was pretty much moved in already. But her lease doesn't officially start until the beginning of the semester, and the landlord won't let her stay over the break because of insurance reasons. So she has to make two trips. Bad timing, is all."

"I thought something was up," Gil said. Neither of them was in the mood to talk much more. They'd made small talk all day with relatives and family friends, some of whom they hadn't seen in years. Their emotions were played out, and they were numb. The quiet was a welcome change. There were things they'd need to address, not the least of which was the small fortune that they just spent on Richard's funeral, and now two sets of plane tickets for Mary, but not right then.

# Chapter 9

Mary Sykes was getting ready to pack her bags to go back home for her winter break from UCLA. She had planned on skipping Thanksgiving, and not making the trip home twice, but her cousin's funeral had required her to make two trips in less than a month. Her professors, while sympathetic, would not let her take final exams online, primarily because she had a senior lab seminar that counted for most of her grade, and that particular exam required her to be in the lab.

The first set of plane tickets to go back for the funeral on short notice had been expensive, and now she was taking the long flight again just a few short weeks later but had managed a much better price. Still, she felt guilty because she knew that her mother and father didn't have a lot of money. They certainly weren't nearly as wealthy as many of her fellow students.

Mary was both an academic and athletic prodigy. She'd broken two state intramural track records when she was a sophomore in high school and had the best of both parts of her mother and father when it came to academic talent. She was quick like her father, but methodical like her mom. Her scholarship took a large chunk out of the tuition, but her parents still supported her, and she was well aware of that. She'd decided that this trip home would be the best time to talk to them about her plans.

While she'd been accepted at several graduate schools, she didn't want to go, at least not yet. Instead she had decided that she wanted to join the Peace Corps. While she knew her mother would understand, she knew her father would probably not like the idea of his little girl going to the Third World to teach English and build schools. He'd mentioned grad school a few times when she was home, and she'd changed the subject. Mary sighed and started to pack her red suitcases.

Most of her friends and both her roommates had already left, so when there was a knock on the door, she was a little surprised. It was Paul from her psychology lab. She'd worked with him on their semester-long project as a lab partner.

"Hi," she said with the door open between them.

"I should have called you but took a chance. Everyone's gone already, but I remembered you saying that you were staying until tomorrow." He smiled and looked down at his feet.

"Oh," she opened the door to let him in. She motioned to a sofa. She hadn't realized how tall he was until he was in her living room, although she remembered that his lab coat was well above his knees. He seemed to always be scrunching down so as to not appear as tall. In her small apartment, on her Salvation Army couch, his knees were above the level of the armrests. "Would you like to sit in the chair instead? Would that be more comfortable?" Mary said, motioning to the black leather lounge chair.

"No, thanks." He leaned forward. "All my height is in my legs. I don't usually fit in any furniture." He grinned. "It's all a little too close to the ground for me. The worst is the real ultra-modern stuff. I can't ever get comfortable in any of it. Too low to the ground and too weird."

"I agree. If I sit in it, I can't get out again." Mary laughed.

"I can see that happening."

"You aren't making references to my height, are you?"

"No, I'd never do that. But you know better than to plan on a career in women's basketball, right?"

"The damage is done. No need to try to make it up," she teased him.

"You certainly run fast enough, though."

"How do you know that?"

"I was at your last track meet."

"I didn't know you knew I ran track."

"You did mention it a few times, that you have a scholarship. A couple of weeks ago I saw you run. One of my roommates is on the men's team, and I've been promising him to go see him since the start of the semester. We got there early and watched the women's team." He took a breath. "You did very well."

"Thanks." She was a little embarrassed, because while she'd used them as an excuse, she'd had some lab absences that weren't really for them. She had stuck him with more than his share of the project but, she consoled herself, she'd done all the real tedious statistics, and he did most of the writing, so they made a good team. But she did take advantage of Paul's sweet nature. In fact, she now remembered using him as a sounding board more than once about her now ex-boyfriend, and about going home for Richard's funeral. He'd been a good listener. When he spent some time telling her about his parent's continual disastrous marriage, she returned the favor of listening, and was smart enough not to offer any advice.

"Cool." There was a long silence. "I should have called."

"No," Mary said. "It's nice you came by. I just finished packing. The plane leaves tomorrow at ten, but you lose three hours going east, so I won't get to New York until late, and then I'll be jet lagged all to shit. I don't travel well."

"All I have to do is drive up the coast for three hours and then I'm home."

"Lucky you."

"You wouldn't say that if you met my family. Why do you think I'm still here at the end of finals week? Hell, I was finished three days ago."

"I remember you talking about them."

"Dysfunctional?"

"Right. You had some wild stories."

"All true. I aced abnormal psych. All I needed to do was to think about my parents." He paused. "I was going to get something to eat. Are you hungry?"

"I think you aced most of your classes," she said. "As a matter of fact, I could eat, but I have to save my cash right now for the trip home."

"My treat, Mary."

"I couldn't take advantage."

"Then buy me a meal when you get back next semester," Paul said. Mary thought it over. She *was* hungry, and there was no food in the house. She and her two roommates had cleaned everything out for the end of the semester.

"Okay. Let me clean up a little. And I will owe you a dinner next year." She left the room and went to the small bathroom to wash up and change her shirt. They walked to a local eatery, a place that was popular with students, but pretty much abandoned now this close to the holiday, which was nice, since they got seated very quickly. Mary looked at the menu, and, although it was reasonably priced, she ordered one of the cheaper items, a salad with seared tuna.

While they waited, she mentioned that she might not be going right to grad school. He smiled and listened to her as she unfolded her plans. As it happened, she talked right through dinner without much let up; all the things she'd planned on saying to her mother and father but couldn't because of the suspension in time that the funeral had created. Her aunt had taken up her mother's energy, and then the rest of Thanksgiving seemed like an emotional vacuum. Paul listened while he ate his burger, and then offered her some of his fries. She said no and continued to talk. As much as she knew she was being selfish, impolite, maybe even inappropriate, by dumping all of it on him, a boy she only knew because of a random assignment for her clinical psych lab, she couldn't stop herself. And Paul listened. Eventually, she stopped, and then apologized.

He smiled. "No problem. We're all nervous about graduating and the future. I still don't know if I'm ready for more school yet, although I have a couple of prospects." He thought for a second. "You might want to talk to my dad. He was in the Peace Corps."

"Really?"

"Yeah. He has a degree in agricultural engineering from Cornell. They took him in a heartbeat. He really got some good experience there, and it helped him get a job when he got out. People think you're a self-starter, entrepreneurial, all that good shit when you volunteer like that."

"Is your dad really like that? I mean community oriented? From what you say of him he's a little …."

"He's an asshole. For him it was either volunteer or take his chances with the draft. He wasn't happy with the idea of possibly ending up in Vietnam, so he signed up."

"Oh."

"Don't get me wrong. He's not an asshole because of that. It's because of how he treats my mom. However, she does enable him, in her own passive aggressive way."

"Does psychology ever help, I wonder?"

"I wonder, too, sometimes. It gives us a way of describing behavior; not sure if it helps anyone change, though. She'll stay with him until the day she dies, and he'll cheat on her, control her money, psychologically abuse and belittle her until then."

"That's sad," she said, remembering the conversations they'd over the semester about his family.

"I told her to divorce him, but she listens to bad advice from her friends. She thinks she'll end up homeless if she leaves him."

"Not in this country, especially not in California. It's not Saudi Arabia."

"That's what I tell her." Paul spread his long fingers out on the table. "Which is why I've come to the conclusion that it's not just him, it's her, too. It's how they have evolved their relationship, how they relate to each other. So you see why I'd rather stay here than go home for the holidays? What about your parents? You never talk about them much."

"Dad, as you know, is an English professor. Mom's an editor. She used to work a lot in New York and I hardly ever saw her. She'd leave about six and come home late, usually after we were in bed. But she stopped after I was eight or so, and since then she works from home. Dad's now threatening to retire, but my guess is he won't, not until Jason graduates at least."

"Do they get along?"

"Yes. They aren't at all into any kind of drama. Although I now realize that there was some tension when she was away all the time. She's very pretty, so I sometimes wonder if Dad was just worried—or jealous." She looked at the artwork on the walls. A local artist was displaying his paintings, seascapes with bleached-white bones arranged as if they were chained together. "They were acting kind of weird at the funeral. I thought it was because of the fact that everything landed on them. He literally had to deal with every detail, and Mom had to take care of Aunt Claudia. My aunt is very needy. It's just her way, and Mom indulges her.

I think Claudia takes advantage, and that causes some tension between them. Dad loses patience with Aunt Claudia. Can't blame her this time. My God, she lost her only son. Her husband was killed in a car accident years ago, so now she's totally alone, and I really wonder if she's strong enough to deal with it." She stopped for a deep breath. "I do think there was something on Dad's mind, though, and it had nothing to do with the funeral."

Now there was silence, as if the opening in time for talking had snapped shut.

"I can spring for an ice cream if you want dessert," Mary said as they rose to leave. "There's a place around the corner. The ice cream is supposed to be like real Italian gelato. It's close, but not really quite there."

"I'd like to go to Italy," Paul said.

"We went for half a year when my dad taught in Florence."

"That must have been cool."

"I was thirteen and had a great time. Didn't want to come back even though we had a small apartment with one bathroom and I had a tiny bedroom, just big enough for a daybed and a small armoire. They have no closets in those old apartments. I also had to keep an eye on my nine-year-old brother. There were no babysitters. And, of course, I fell in love with the place, and with a boy."

Paul opened the door for her, and they walked out into the cool evening.

"Italian?"

"Not exactly. He was the son of the visiting history professor. They were from England, Oxford." She smiled. "That's my speed, good old Mary goes to Italy and falls in love with an Englishman. Man, did I carry on like an idiot when he left and we had to go back to the States. I think I wrote him every day for a couple of months. I was inconsolable. But he didn't write back as much as I wrote to him, and it wasn't the same. I needed to hear his voice. I couldn't get enough of his accent. I'd ask him questions just to hear him talk. I think he finally caught on, though."

"I could see you doing that."

"Because I'm so deceptive?"

"No."

"Sorry. I've been talking about me all night."

"That's okay. You had to vent. Much more stress and you might have exploded." He smiled.

"That would have made a mess. It's not polite to explode when someone takes you out to dinner."

They walked to the ice cream shop. It, too, was empty. A bored clerk made up their order, and they went outside and sat at a picnic table. The air was cooler now, and there was a strong breeze from Santa Monica. It was a bit too nippy to eat ice cream, but neither of them minded. Mary got a chill as they walked back to her place, then she looked up at Paul and kissed him. He had to bend down to reach her mouth.

"I just broke up with someone, and have no intention of having another boyfriend," she said.

"I know, and I'm not looking for a girlfriend. My life is already complicated."

"Good. Then come on up."

When they got to her apartment, she took the bags off her bed and put them in the living room. She had already made arrangements for a cab to pick her up the next morning. They went into her bedroom, sat on her bed and kissed for a while; then they started to take off their clothes. She paused for a moment while undoing her bra, noticing that with his clothes off, Paul was even skinnier that he looked with them on. She could see his thigh bones framing thick dark pubic hair and his penis like two butterfly wings, and he really was all legs, long skinny legs. He was looking at her, too. She liked that but was self-conscious about her small breasts that her mom had wrongly promised would grow bigger someday. Her ex-boyfriend, who had put on so much weight during their last year together that it hurt her breasts when they had sex, had almost never looked at her.

Paul was a lot lighter, and much gentler. His skin felt cool to the touch as they fondled each other. He entered her slowly, and took his time; he also lasted a lot longer, long enough for her to finish, too, and she came harder than she had in a long time, as if she were flushing out all the stress and emotions that had built up, flushing out her soul. His hips, though, dug painfully into her sides when he sank down into her, and she had to push him off to the side. She stroked his long hair.

"You need to put some meat on your bones. Don't you ever eat?"

"I get too busy to eat sometimes."

"I wish I could say that."

"You are not at all fat. In fact, you have what they call a hard-body, probably from all that running, and your legs are really strong."

"So you're an expert on women's bodies?" she teased.

"Mostly theoretical," he said, and she could feel him blushing even in the dark.

"I have to get up early, a long day of hurry-up-and-wait. Luckily, I got a nonstop flight."

"I'll go," he said.

"No rush." She paused for a time, staring at the ceiling dimly lit by the hall light, looking at the swirling patterns that someone had put on it with a thick layer of joint compound to hide all the cracks in the plaster, probably from the various earthquakes.

"Look, Paul, why don't we see each other every now and then? Nothing romantic; we'll be going our separate ways in a few months anyway. Just benefits, you know, dinner together, a movie, you know."

"Sure," he said. "We're both pretty busy, though."

She thought for a minute. "Thursdays?"

"What?"

"I'm free Thursdays from three on. It's like the only day I don't have many classes or work, and there usually is no practice for the track team."

"I think I'm free, too."

"Great. Thursdays it is," she said, "unless I have a track meet."

"Maybe I'll come, too, and cheer you on."

"You don't have to."

"We'll see," he said, and kissed her. She stroked him, and he was ready again; she didn't resist, but insisted on taking top to avoid his razor hips. Paul left an hour later.

Mary took a cab to the airport the next morning and flew home.

# Chapter 10

Gil was in his office reading a short story published that month in Harper's, one of those stories where the point of view shifted even though it was supposed to be the same person. Obviously, the writer was a graduate of an MFA program, but not one that was so prestigious that it ruined her as a writer; it just made her strange and purposely quirky. Gil was getting fed up with the clever writerly tricks at the same time the story ended, so it was indeed a draw.

The fall semester had come to a rapid end right after Richard's funeral and then Thanksgiving. Marion had been right. The funeral eclipsed what had been for them a family holiday that had always meant getting together and having some special time together. It had been a welcome breather before the brutal attack of Christmas and all that it entailed.

He was waiting for the stragglers to turn in their final papers. The deadline was in a few minutes, and two students still hadn't dropped off or emailed them to him. One wasn't a surprise, but the other one had been Edith Frank. Even though she was only sixteen, she was better than most of the students in his class, so he wasn't sure what to make of her missing the deadline. If anything, she'd consistently handed her assignments in early. As if in answer to his question, Edith was suddenly in his doorway. Her disheveled hair was several shades of pastel colors, which was nothing unusual, but she seemed uncommonly distracted.

"Sorry, Professor Sykes," she said, handing him her final paper.

"Nothing to be sorry about. You're on time, just, but you made it." Gil smiled. He took her paper and put it on the bottom of the pile in front of him.

"I just got a little behind."

"I understand."

"Some things came up, and I got a little overwhelmed."

"I'm just glad you handed it in. You've always been a good student, so if you had a serious, valid reason for not being on time, I would certainly have given you an extension."

"No. It was just stupid. I did something really stupid." Edith was suddenly very pale, and started to cry, but succeeded in holding back. Gil instinctively reached out to her. She took his hand, and then burst into tears, leaning against him. He held her, and she shook while she sobbed. When she started to settle down, he asked if she was all right. She let go of his hand and nodded. She backed away and smiled at him, embarrassed. "Sorry, Professor Sykes. I've been under a lot of strain."

"Let me know if I can help." Gil hesitated a moment before saying, "We have counselors if you need to talk to someone."

"Talk might not help me too much right now," she said quickly, making a visible effort to pull herself together. "Thanks, Professor. Sorry I got all emotional." She had switched from scared teenager back to being a student. "I'm okay now." Her smile looked more to Gil like a painful grimace. She went down the hall and took the stairs, not noticing Gary Sime, Administrative Vice Provost, who had listened to the whole exchange while lurking in the hallway.

Gil made a note to send an email to the Advising Center and see if they could do some outreach for Edith.

He gave the remaining wayward student— who came late, was never really present, and smelled of alcohol and pot most of the time—a full hour grace period before packing his briefcase and leaving. Gil shook his head at the thought of the money someone was laying out for the kid to take up a seat at Bradbury. He thought perhaps it would have been cheaper to rent him a hotel room for fifteen weeks and let him party until he got it out of his system.

Gil didn't relish the idea of reading through the stack of essays. He'd already graded a few, but when he'd read the line, "Moby Dick is a floating metaphor," he'd chuckled, put that paper carefully away, and began reading his magazine. *Indeed it is a floating metaphor. A swimming and diving one, too.*

He checked his email one last time and found a note from Val. The mental exercise of working on her article had helped him get past Richard's funeral. It also forced him to go back to some of his academic roots. A careful and thorough scholar, Gil was also a careful writer, and would rework a sentence numerous times until he was satisfied that it said exactly what he wanted it to say. Valerie had sent him her presentation from the conference, and he had been rewriting large sections, promising to work more over the break, as soon as he finished grading the finals.

Her email said she was just connecting with him to see how things were coming along. Gil smiled and sent her a reply. She wrote back to him asking if he was in his office. After he said yes, his phone rang.

"Hi, Gil," she said as he picked up.

"Hi, Val."

"I wanted to thank you for protecting me. You stood between me and the nut-jobs." She laughed. "I'm not sure who was more scary, the people who liked what I said or the people who hated it."

"Just wait until after it's published, then you'll have plenty of people to deal with who don't like what you have to say."

"You think so?"

"People will resent what they see as another attack on a founding father, patriotism, and all that's American."

"But it's the truth," Valerie protested.

"That's beside the point. The truth is never enough, not when it flies in the face of folklore." "There will be some reaction to this. Remember when they had DNA evidence that Jefferson had fathered children with Sally Hemings?"

"That didn't go over too well," Valerie said. "They'd have rather found out he was a pedophile." She chose her next words carefully. "I heard about your nephew. It must have been terrible. I'm sure it was an ordeal. I probably should have waited a while before sending you those pages. If you had taken a break from working on this, I would have understood."

"I'm glad you did send them. Whenever I'm stressed, the best thing for me is to work. I didn't take offense or anything. I welcomed the distraction."

"I think we can set some sort of record getting this article published," Valerie said.

They small-talked for a few more minutes, and then wished each other a happy holiday. Gil hung up the phone, checked the time, and left his office. A student essay flopped on his office rug when he opened his door; it had been leaning against the kick plate. The prodigal student had managed to turn something in after all.

*\*\**

Marion had no work at the moment. There was a book in the pipeline about the latest research in brain imaging technology and depression, and she was happy to wait for that one. She was getting the house ready for the holidays and trying to avoid her sister. She felt guilty, but she was burnt out from dealing with her, and couldn't spare the energy required to be an emotional crutch.

While in the attic getting some decorations and the artificial tree she'd bought several years ago after they'd had a couple of disasters with natural trees, she looked out the window. She'd always had the notion to move their bedroom up here and make an en suite with a walk-in closet, a master bedroom suite that ran the length of the house. She actually could see a small strip of the Hudson from the attic window. And it was quiet. There were no street noises, and no sound of barking dogs. But there'd never been enough money for such a renovation.

The artificial tree was in its own case, and not very heavy. The last real tree they had was so bad that the needles fell off before New Year's Eve, and Gil took it down because it had become a fire hazard. They joked that it was a "Charlie Brown" Christmas tree. She'd found herself vacuuming up pine needles until March. So when she saw a nice artificial tree on sale at local grocery store that called itself a "farmer's market," she bought it, and loaded it into the car. It had taken her a couple of hours to set it up for the first time, but now a few minutes was all she needed to straighten out the branches and then it was ready for the ornaments.

Gil had helped with the tree when they were first married, but now it was entirely up to her, as was pretty much everything else that concerned the house, the kids, or anything domestic. To be honest, though, he did take charge of the funeral and all the many details.

She was excited that Mary and Jason were going to both be home. Mary had stayed in California the previous year to spend the holidays with her boyfriend and his family, only to decide to break up with him this year, which Marion had suspected was going to happen probably before her daughter did. From her point of view, it had never been a good match anyway, but Marion had carefully stayed out of it.

And while she was going to work hard to keep Richard's death from spoiling the holiday, she also felt obligated to invite Claudia for dinner on Christmas. Gil, in his passive aggressive way, had left it up to her, although she knew he'd hate to have to deal with Claudia over the holidays.

Her thoughts drifted back to that horrible day when she'd gotten the news of Richard's death. Lost in memory, she dropped an ornament, and it shattered on the hardwood floor.

"Damn." Sweeping up the broken glass, she wondered how Gil could manage to be away every time there was a crisis. Maybe that was unfair, she chided herself, but it seemed like he was good at being out of town, or very busy when something went wrong, as if he had a sixth sense and knew when to make himself scarce.

She finished trimming the tree and checked the time. Gil would be home late because of a meeting; Jason was supposed to drive home that afternoon after his last exam; and Mary would be home in a couple of days. She knew that she shouldn't depend so much on her kids being part of her life. They were both adults, and very soon would probably move away. She knew it in her head, but it wasn't part of her emotional knowing.

Her cell rang: Claudia. Marion had let two of her calls go to voicemail at the house phone, so she probably assumed she was out and called her cell.

Marion sighed and pushed the button to accept the call.

"Hi, Claudia."

"Marion. Where are you?"

"Home."

"Well, I called twice, but there was no answer."

"I must have been outside and didn't hear the phone."

"In this weather?"

"What's up, Claudia?"

"I was going to ask you to go out for lunch."

"I'm not in the mood for pizza."

"I was going to take you to Gino's, smartass," Claudia said. Gino's was Marion's favorite restaurant.

"In that case, I'll meet you there. What time?"

"It's almost one now."

"Really?" Marion looked at the clock. "Okay. Then I'll wash up and meet you there in about twenty minutes?"

"Sure. I'll see you in twenty minutes."

Gino's had once been a German restaurant that had some pretty mediocre food. After more than one instance of suspicious food poisoning, the owners put the place up for sale and one of the adjunct professors at the college, Gino Russo, took out a home equity loan and bought it. He was a talented cook who had decided that the area could use a decent Italian place. He'd been right. In a short time, he was grossing about as much in a month as he had made teaching for a whole year. He still taught as a hobby but could not afford the cut in pay to do it very often. The food was a mix of modern Italian cuisine and traditional "red-sauce" entrees. When Marion and Claudia got there, much of the lunch crowd was already gone. There were tables where people were lingering over desserts or drinks, but the restaurant was quiet.

They placed their orders and nibbled on breadsticks while waiting to be served.

"I wanted to thank you, and Gil, too, for all the help you were during Richard's ...."

"It's okay. And Gil did most of the work, really."

"Really? I thought he hated me," Claudia said.

"No. He actually likes you."

"How can you tell?"

"There's a subtle difference, but it's there," Marion said. She wanted to add that he even had liked Richard and was disappointed when things hadn't worked out for him at Bradbury, but she knew better than to mention him at all right now and was surprised that Claudia had managed to say his name and not fall to pieces.

Marion noticed the dilated pupils—Claudia also had ordered an unusually large amount of food—and wondered if she was on an antidepressant.

Their meals arrived, and Marion focused on eating, but listened to Claudia, who was even more talkative and willing to overshare than normal. Claudia lived her life in public and needed input and approval from others. In many ways, she was Marion's opposite.

"We're having our usual Christmas dinner," Marion said. "We'll be eating early, about four. Jason wants to go to his friend's house to watch football." She sipped her wine.

"I'll think about it. My husband's family invited me, too. I've been leaning on you too much and I know it. Maybe I'll go there instead," Claudia replied.

Marion sat back for a minute and thought. The polite thing would be to make the offer again.

"Not a problem," she said instead. "I'm sure you'll have a nice time there."

"You and Gil must had have had enough of me by now."

"No. Not at all," Marion replied.

Claudia was thoughtful, and quiet for the first time all afternoon, as if wrestling with something, trying to find the words.

"You know," she said, "Richard did go to Bradbury for a while."

"One semester as I recall," Marion commented, then regretted her tone. "Sorry."

"I'm not stupid. I know he lied a lot about where he was and what he was really doing," Claudia said, "but he did mention something I need to share with you." She bit her lip before saying, "He mentioned that Gil sometimes gets a bit too friendly with his female students."

"Really? And he based this accusation on?"

"Just what he heard."

"From?"

"I don't know, he just mentioned it to me one day when we were talking." Claudia said apologetically. "It might explain why he made sure your two kids didn't go to Bradbury."

"Our kids went where they got scholarships," Marion said, her voice flat.

"Sorry I brought it up."

"It's okay. As you already said, Richard did have problems telling the truth." She looked at her watch, and Claudia got the hint. She paid the bill and Marion insisted on leaving the tip. They went to the parking lot and quickly hugged goodbye. Marion sat in the parking lot for a minute before starting her car and driving to the store before going home.

# Chapter 11

Gil was in his home office finishing up grading final papers and assessing final grades. He was surprised that Edith Frank's paper had had so many errors, but it was fundamentally sound, so he gave her the benefit of the doubt. It wasn't the first time he'd had a gifted student have issues near the end of the semester. The rest of the grades were pretty predictable. The boy who'd handed the final essay in so late had obviously not read any of the books, nor paid a lot of attention in class. It had been a hodgepodge of plagiarized material from the internet with glaring inaccuracies that came either from an uninformed internet source or from the student. It didn't really matter at this point.

Gil wondered if students thought that professors were so out of touch that they didn't know how to find information on the internet, or that there even was an internet. It was an attitude he'd run into more than once, and he thought it was probably from the current popular culture with its generous dose of anti-intellectualism, the bizarre notion that somehow a person who had studied a subject for many years and written books about it didn't know as much as a loudmouth with a TV show who plays to the camera. In any case, the student failed, and Gil had the feeling that he would hear from his parents.

Jason poked his head in the office door.

"Hi, Dad."

"Hi," Gil said, closing his gradebook and putting the papers on his desk into stacks.

"All done?"

"Yes. Just have to post the grades tomorrow morning. I'll probably take a walk, though."

"Good." Jason hesitated.

"What's up?"

"I was just getting ready to drive to the airport and get Mary. Mom asked me just before she went out this morning."

Gil looked at his watch. "You have plenty of time. She won't be there for a couple of hours yet. It shouldn't take that long to get there. They also have the slowest baggage claim on the planet."

"That's true." There was a long silence as Gil finished putting the papers on the desk. "So I was wondering …."

"If I could go get your sister?"

"Yeah, Dad, I want to go to Ray's this afternoon. He just got back last night and some of us are getting together."

"That's fine. I feel like getting out anyway. I need to decompress; been cooped up for a few days with those papers. I'll take my walk later, after I get back."

"Thanks, Dad."

"You will remember to be around sometime this break, Jason? Your mom will be very angry if you skip out for the entire time you're home."

"I will. Thanks again, Dad." Jason left, and Gil heard him backing down the driveway. He made himself a cup of coffee and looked around for his keys. In a little over an hour, he was on the highway to the airport. The new arrivals section had conformed to the current security rules, which did not allow anyone to park near the terminal exit. He was a little early and didn't feel like driving in circles waiting for Mary to emerge, so he parked in the short-term lot and walked to the baggage claim area. No one was there yet. He leaned against a tourist information kiosk while people drifted into the area and lined up around the turntable. He spotted her coming down the escalator and was astonished at how much she seemed a young version of her mother. He waved. She looked at him, and then waved back with a big smile.

"Hi, Dad." she hugged him and kissed him on the cheek.

"Hi. You look good. How was the flight?"

"I managed to sleep most of the way." She smiled. "I remembered these for a change." She reached into her handbag and pulled out a set of earplugs, a sleep mask, and a small container of cannabis lozenges. "There are always screaming kids on that flight, so you gotta take precautions."

"Smart," Gil said. "Just put the cannabis away while you're in New York. You might run into an overzealous police officer."

They waited for her much-used red bags, and then Gil wheeled them to his car and put them the trunk. They drove out of the airport and to the highway. The white landscape looked stark from the highway, and the backyards of people as they drove past housing projects offered a depressing mix of covered grills, frozen swimming pools, and snowbound swing sets.

"I'm beginning to like California more and more every time I come home."

"You mean you don't miss the change of season?"

"Nope," Mary replied. "Especially when it changes to a meat freezer." She gave him a quick look before saying, "We are fundamentally meat, you know? Warm meat."

"A bit reductive, don't you think?"

"Not when it gets cold out. Then it's obvious."

"Okay. I'll let it go." He smiled, glad to see she had her sense of humor back. "You seem to be in a better mood than you were last month."

"Got rid of some things that were bothering me."

"Your mom told me."

"About?"

"Your boyfriend? I guess he's now your ex?"

"Yeah," she said, relieved. "He was too dependent. I couldn't deal with his passive aggressive crap anymore." She thought for a moment. "I think I must have gotten him a dozen free tickets to my track meets before I realized he wasn't going to show up, ever. Then when I gave the complimentary tickets to my friends, who actually did come to the meet, he got all kinds of angry with me. I pointed out the fact that he never showed up anyway, and it was a waste of the tickets when I had a lot of friends who actually *wanted* to come to the track meets. He reminded me that the tickets were free, which was beside the point, right? And then he decided to let me know women only got sports scholarships because the school needed women to meet their quota in sports. That's when I blew up at him."

Gil's laugh sounded more like a bark. "Really? Didn't he realize you won the state championships three years running? Was he that bad? He seemed nice when I met him."

"He was nice two years ago, then he became an asshole. I guess I never noticed his manipulative behavior, but it finally occurred to me that he never actually did anything he told me he was going to do, or if he did finally manage, he was late, or inappropriate. Even if it was just going out to meet some friends for a pizza, he'd say it was fine, and he'd be there, but he'd invariably show up an hour late and dressed in his sweats. He also was the absolute master of having an elaborate dinner ready on the same night I had a late practice, or had to be in the lab, or go to a mandatory guest lecture, so he could make sure I let him down by not being home on time, when he knew full well I would be late." She looked out the window. They were getting near their exit. "I don't know what I want to do with my life, and everything is about to get very serious in a few months. I guess I simply don't have time for dealing with passive aggressive, or any bullshit."

"I know. It's a scary time." Gil agreed. "You want to hold off on grad school, your mom said?"

Mary stared at her dad, and then squeezed his arm. If he hadn't been driving, she would have hugged him. "Just for now. I want to see some of what's out there. I was thinking of the Peace Corps."

"I figured as much. Not the Peace Corps part. I still have to think about that. When I graduated, I'd only planned on taking a little time off before going back to school, but it's harder that way, and harder than you think. If it weren't for your mother pushing me, I might not have gone back to school at all. After I got my degree and got a job, then it was my turn to push her to finish hers. We helped each other over the years. I was changing your diapers while she went to night school." He grinned. "What I'm saying is that it's okay to take a little time off—they call it a gap year now—but it can be really hard to go back once you're out, especially if you get a job or start a family. You might not ever go back to school, and that would be a shame."

"I know, Dad. One school said they would allow for delayed admission, but I'd lose any financial aid, and they couldn't guarantee me anything after about a year. Peace Corps wants twenty-seven months."

"That long? Maybe you could find some program that lasts a year or so? Maybe you could get a position where you could teach English or intern overseas in psychology or something like that? You liked Italy as I remember. Or was it that boy?"

"Sure. I'm checking out all my options. Nothing is set yet. And I thought you had no idea I had a crush."

"I might be a little preoccupied, but I'm not totally unconscious." Gil laughed. "You were overcome with grief, pining around the house, heaving deep sighs, bursting into tears."

"Dad!"

"Okay. You did get over him eventually."

"Yes, I did." She looked out the window and noticed that they had much more snow than had been at the airport. "At least we'll have a white Christmas."

# Chapter 12

Gil was looking through his notes while students sauntered in. Peter Morton, his teaching assistant, came in with the rest of the students. He usually went to the back of the room, and, after the start of the semester, would take about half the class in a discussion group once a week. Peter greeted Gil, whom he hadn't seen since the break began, and they made an appointment to talk after class about logistics.

Gil turned to go to the front of the class when he noticed that Edith Frank, who was quite pale to begin with, was perfectly white. In fact, her skin was transparent; he could see the veins in her face and the freckles on her nose.

"Are you feeling okay, Ms. Frank?" Gil asked.

Edith looked at him, her deep blue eyes glistening with tears, and then she vomited on her desk and fell off her chair in a dead faint.

Gil stooped down quickly and caught her just before she hit her head on the concrete floor. One of the students called 911, then announced that the campus ambulance was on the way. A security guard quickly materialized in the doorway of the classroom. Gil had elevated Edith's feet, and turned her head in case she were to vomit again. Another security guard came in the classroom with a first-aid kit, but the paramedics had already arrived, so he didn't open it.

By then, Edith had come back to consciousness. It took a moment before she realized she was on the floor.

"Oh, my God. Did I pass out?"

"How are you feeling now?" the first paramedic asked while looking at her pupils with a small flashlight. The other took her blood pressure. "Are you dizzy?"

Edith nodded.

"Her BP is low, and she's cyanotic under her fingernails and around her lips. I'll give her some oxygen," the second paramedic said while opening a mask and hooking it up to the tank on the gurney.

"Did you eat anything today?" the first paramedic asked, having continually dealt with the persistent epidemic of anorexia and bulimia among young women, which made an eating disorder her first logical diagnosis, but the blue fingernails had her very concerned. Could be pneumonia. Edith shook her head.

The first paramedic looked up. "Let's start an IV and give her some glucose." She turned to Edith. We're going to have to put a needle in your hand, Edith, and then we are going to take you to the emergency room."

"No," Edith said almost inaudibly.

"You can refuse, but I really think you need to see a doctor," the paramedic said.

"No," she said again, even more weakly, but then passed out, her face covered in sweat. The first paramedic looked at the second, her eyebrows raised.

"She looks as if she's going into shock. This is more than skipping a couple of meals," she said. The paramedics got the IV started, strapped Edith to a gurney, took her out of the building, and headed for the local hospital with lights and siren. A custodian showed up to mop up the small puddle of vomit on the floor and to clean the desk. Gil had picked up Edith's books; she'd managed to miss them when she vomited. He put them on his desk and would keep them for her in his office until she got back to school. Gil let class out early because no one was paying the slightest bit of attention anyway. By now all cell phones and social media sites related to anything on campus had been brought up to date about the incident in class, complete with photos of Edith passed out on the floor of the classroom with Gil holding her head, and two paramedics hovering over her. She was so pale she looked as if she could be dead.

***

Edith woke up in a hospital room feeling better; the emergency room physician had given her an examination and the cause of her distress became obvious, so she wanted to keep her overnight for observation. The doctor did not tell Mrs. Frank about the abortion.

Luckily, she didn't have any complications, only low blood sugar from not eating and even lower electrolytes from dehydration. The doctor thought it was miraculous that she had even made it to class.

Her mother was at the foot of the bed.

"So, Edith, what's going on?"

"I'm not sure what you mean, Mom."

"Enough." In her courtroom voice, she addressed her daughter. "You've been a nervous wreck since the end of the school year. Do you think I'm an idiot? That I don't notice things? Now, tell me what's going on."

Edith burst into tears. Her mother waited patiently, and then Edith told her most of what happened.

# Chapter 13

Gil checked his mail and found a padded envelope from the literary journal that published Val's article. He opened it in his office and saw that her article, "A Small Matter of Plagiarism," was the lead article. He was listed in the acknowledgments.

"Wow," Gil said. While he had already read several versions of the article, including the final draft, he sat down to read it in hard copy. There was something about a published article that seemed to give it an authority or legitimacy, even if you wrote it and know exactly what's in it. This would be a seminal piece in the field. He sent Valerie an email congratulating her. His cell phone rang immediately.

"Hello."

"Hi, Gil, it's Val. Got your email. It's very sweet. Thanks."

"Thanks for listing me first in the acknowledgements and giving me all that praise. It might go to my head."

"You rewrote over half of it. In any case, it's done. It's out there."

"I'm sure you'll get a rational measured response."

"From whom?"

"You're right. The melodrama will be insane."

"And, Gil, they're talking about a book, and I'm going to need help. You're going to help me, right?" Valerie said.

"Not a problem. Let's wait and see."

"You're right. No need to look for trouble. Okay. I'll keep in touch, and I'll send you my schedule so we can have lunch."

***

The article inspired the usual number of comments— few—which was normal for any academic work. Sasha Korbet, however, was one of the people who read the article. As a reporter for the local paper, she read it simply because it listed a local professor at Bradbury in the acknowledgements. Sasha remembered breaking two stories about sexual harassment covered up by the school the previous year. There was one involving a professor, and the other involved a basketball player. There was a sudden tightness in her stomach when she remembered how the administration at Bradbury had stonewalled her on both cases. She'd expected it, but they hadn't counted on her getting information from an insider. The story was picked up by the wire services and went nationwide. After that, one of the members of Bradbury's board had tried to get her fired and came very close to succeeding. The only thing that had saved her job was the fact that her article had come out at exactly the same time the video of an enraged coach screaming at the victim hit social media, and a short clip of that video, over the past year, had even become a meme for the false righteous indignation and emotion in plentiful supply on social media.

Sasha read Val's article with interest, and then wrote a short piece on it, basically hitting the highlights. She meant it as pretty much a fluff piece that might embarrass the college a little, and she knew that it would score points with her bosses. Any article that involved college professors challenging the reputation of a founding father, the conservative conglomerate that owned the newspaper was only too happy to run in the string of newspapers it owned, and it even leaked over to a five-second blurb on a couple of TV stations.

It took about eight weeks before members of the talk radio circuit, white supremacist/alt right blogs, and neo-Nazi fan clubs became scandalized and worked themselves up to be sufficiently apoplectic for the more mainstream conservative media to notice the essay. As it had been a slow news cycle, the talking heads were looking for something to land on to boost ratings. Then pieces of the essay completely devoid of context were published in conservative and then mainstream newspapers and news magazines, and then it reached the tipping point where it hit social media like a storm. Most of the articles were very critical and had headlines like, "Elitist Liberal Academics Accuse Thomas Jefferson of Theft!" or "Article Claims that a Black Pirate wrote the Declaration of Independence!"

Val's tiny liberal arts college, Chamberlain, was featured more than once in the news, as was Bradbury. Needless to say, neither's administration was happy about the publicity.

*** 

Patrick Henri had been a mediocre journalist who had changed his name to that of a famous patriot, gravitated to the talk show circuit, and then managed to move on to cable news where he fed his audience a daily dose of thinly veiled racism, sexism, homophobia, and other raw meat. He was in the office of the cable network programing director who was scrutinizing a spreadsheet on his computer monitor.

"Sorry, Patrick, but your ratings have tanked in the past few months. For God's sake, you polled less than five hundred thousand viewers last week." He pointed to a line on the spreadsheet. "What gives?"

"No idea. Maybe it's that new producer I've got. She isn't pulling her weight."

"Bullshit, Patrick. You're talking to me. No excuses. She came from MTV, she knows her stuff, and you need to learn to get along with her. But that's not the problem."

"What is then?" He sighed. Since he couldn't blame anyone else, which was his primary tactic, he resorted to his fallback approach: sullenness.

"You need to get people watching so we can sell time. That's how we pay the bills. You know that, right?" the director said. "We are in the business of selling commercial time. Don't forget it. Entertainment drives the numbers, and the numbers sell time. You can't lose any more sponsors."

Patrick left the programming director's office, and went to his own office a few floors down, which was next to his studio. The most current newspapers and magazines were on his desk. He usually left it up to his interns to go through them, but today he picked up one of the papers and read a short article by Sasha Korbet that had been syndicated in a number of newspapers. He wasted no time in getting on his laptop and writing the opening monologue; in a matter of minutes, he'd worked himself into a very convincing—and convenient—indignation.

After Patrick Henri brought it to the attention of his audience, talk show hosts and opinion mongers all weighed in on Val's article. Most of them had never read it, and none had read the whole piece. It was an academic article written for an academic audience, so many of the people who read it did not have the stamina to read through all the arguments or nuanced claims, but they did get the idea that Thomas Jefferson might have not originally come up with some of the phrases and ideas that he had used in the Declaration of Independence, or even some that made it into the Constitution.

That was more than enough for the popular press to run with.

Talk radio and the conservative TV new entertainment shows led by Patrick Henri denounced Valerie as unpatriotic and a blame-America-first academic, an intellectual snob who simply didn't understand what a privilege it was to live in the U.S. The more liberal press pointed out that the scholarship was strong; they were fine with one more article pointing to the fundamental racism of a founding father ripping off the ideas of a black man, although their own brand of institutional racism made them hesitate to give too much credit to a black pirate who had been an ex-slave, so they managed to make light of the main claim of the paper. Only the African American community seemed to be completely happy about the whole issue, although the irony was not lost on many of the civil rights leaders.

Even Lenny Trout, author of *Politics and Correctness*, who was now a public intellectual with a column that ran in several papers, weighed in. Trout, whose career was far past its heyday, had jumped on their article and pointed out that there was no real "smoking gun," as if this were a profound criticism and not something Valerie and Gil had both admitted to both at the start of the essay and had included it in the preface to the book that was in progress. Any connection between Jefferson and the captured and enslaved captain of the *Rogue Noir* had to be assumed and would require a little bit of speculation and deduction.

Gil suspected that Trout simply wanted to insert himself in some controversy to see if some of his books might start selling again.

***

June brought unusually warm and muggy weather to the Hudson Valley. Gil mused about the weather either being like a meat locker or steam sauna with little in between. They had all recently returned from Mary's graduation in Los Angeles, and she was busy buying clothes and packing to go to the Netherlands. She had gotten a one-year appointment to teach English at the University of Amsterdam to graduate students in psychology, and she would begin her own graduate work in psychology the following year. Jason had elected to stay in his apartment in Albany and work over the summer at his part-time job. Gil thought it might be best if he spent some time away from home to spread his wings, but, like all parents of young men, had a nagging concern that wouldn't quite let go no matter how much he tried to rationalize it away. Marion had put it very bluntly: "He can get into as much mischief there as here, so what difference does it make?"

With an almost empty house, he'd have plenty of time to work on the book manuscript Valerie had sent him. They spoke on the phone at least every other day to catch up on their progress or met for lunch at a diner about halfway between their homes. They managed to not talk about the publicity about her article. Gil knew that Valerie had been under continual stress from the board of directors of Chamberlain College who'd been under pressure to fire her by influential alums, many of them from rich, white, conservative families. Valerie had spent the bulk of her life in academia, so was not well prepared to talk to journalists, many of whom asked foolish questions with a deadpan look of earnestness.

He worked for a couple of hours. The phone rang, and Gil tried to ignore it. When someone started to leave a long message, he at first thought it was Claudia, but then realized it wasn't so he listened. It was a reporter from News! Magazine, an online news source that had a good reputation for quality journalism. She said she'd noticed that Gil was listed as the co-author of the forthcoming book. She wanted to do a story on Val but couldn't get hold of her. She'd like to include him, too, if he could convince Val. She shared some sample questions that were actually pertinent to the essay.

As a way of explaining how Jefferson could have seen the Charter, they had speculated that he might have met and had a liaison with a slave girl at Tuckahoe Plantation who was the daughter of the captured captain of the *Rogue Noir*. This conjecture made sense in light of the Sally Hemings affair.

Since the press had little time for nuance, there was a lot of talk about Jefferson's sex life, none of which were in the essay or the book. The idea that this was a theory based on fact was lost on the talk show mob. Theirs was a world of titillation and innuendo; carefully reasoned arguments did not make good copy. The reporter left her cell number, twice.

"At least she read the article to the end," Gil said, while dismissing the idea of an interview as absurd. He worked through the morning, only stopping briefly when Marion came in. She had a bag of groceries with her and a small bag of clothes. She'd been buying little things for Mary to take with her to Europe, even though Mary insisted she could easily buy them when she got there. It was Marion's way of adjusting to the idea that her girl was going away.

Gil worked for another hour. He went to the kitchen to get some lunch and was staring at the contents of the refrigerator when his wife came into the kitchen.

"You need to make up your mind. Can't pay to cool off the whole house with the refrigerator." She winked at him. "Isn't that what you always said to the kids?"

"Mostly to Jason. It was like he was studying for an exam the way he'd stare into the fridge," Gil said as he took out some cold cuts. "You want a sandwich?"

"Sure."

"Did you see Claudia at all?"

"No, but I expect she'll call pretty soon. It's been a week."

"Okay," Gil said as he put together sandwiches on a hard roll left over from the intimate graduation party they'd had for Mary the previous week. As Gil ate his sandwich, he and Marion talked about the usual issues including Jason and his friends, especially the ones who seem to think that living at home and playing video games was an acceptable profession.

"There actually are some people, mostly young men, who make a living testing video games, and in video game competitions," Gil said.

"Not many, though, would be my guess."

"Probably not," Gil said. "At least he hasn't come home with that idea yet."

"He'll find his way," Marion assured him.

Gil was getting ready to bite into his sandwich when the phone rang again. The caller ID identified another reporter from yet another news service, an internet-based blog site famous for breaking fresh stories, although they had the bad habit of getting things completely wrong. That didn't seem to affect their readership, or their reputation, though.

The message left was fairly muddled, as he seemed to think that Gil had written the article and was married to Valerie Dymond, and that it was about Jefferson and Sally Hemings. He finished his sandwich.

Marion looked at him. "Should we just unplug the phone?"

"No."

"This has got to stop. Some of these guys are frightening."

Marion was right. Only about half the callers were reporters. The other half were from either very scary fans who wanted to stop over to meet Gil and Valerie—most seemed to assume they lived together—and the others were even scarier self-described patriots, sovereign-state or militia members who wanted to shoot him, Val, his children, and their dog, blow up his car, burn down his house; the solutions ignorant people resort to when their world view is challenged. He had reported the death threats to the local police. They came in and did a threat assessment, then installed a phone tracing device on their home phone, which was basically advanced caller ID. They didn't consider the threats to be credible. Gil wasn't sure.

The threatening calls usually came from blocked numbers, and Gil had set his phone to reject the blocked calls, which did slow them down a lot. The self-appointed patriots weren't so stupid that they would call from their own exchanges. Gil picked up his house phone, dialed the number of the reporter from News! The reporter answered on the second ring.

"This is Gil Sykes. I'm returning your call."

"Yes, June Arbor from News! Magazine. I've been trying to get hold of Valerie Dymond to ask a few questions, but she isn't answering her phone, and then I noticed that you were listed in the acknowledgements, so I took a chance that you might be willing to answer a few questions."

"That depends on the questions," Gil said.

"Sure, of course, I wanted to know about the documents that led to your conclusions."

"They came from an abandoned house that was unearthed in the major earthquake in 2010."

"So there was no hint of this document before then?"

"No, not that I'm aware of."

"And you and Valerie seem to feel that there is a connection at Tuckahoe Plantation to the young Jefferson."

"Yes, he would have had access."

"To whom?"

"At least to the captain of the pirate ship who became his cousin's slave," Gil said.

"Lenny Trout pointed out that you have a big gap here."

"We admitted to the gap already in the first paragraph. You just need to use a bit of imagination. Marcus, the enslaved captain, had a daughter who would have been in her teens. She was also noted for her beauty, but you have to remember, young Jefferson would also have had access to Marcus."

"Would they normally have had conversation?"

"Not really, but Jefferson was unusual himself when it came to race relations in the 1700s. In any case, it's quite a coincidence that the two crossed paths and the wording of the pirate Charter is so close to the wording of the Declaration of Independence. That's pretty much our argument," Gil said.

The reporter asked a few more questions and some for background regarding how long he'd been teaching, how long he'd known Val, if they'd worked together before, mostly to round out the article.

\*\*\*

It had taken some convincing to make sure that Mary went ahead with her plans. Once she heard about the threats, she was going to resign her job, but Marion prevailed. There were plenty of nuts in the country who were harmless, she argued; there was no need to worry. Mary wasn't entirely convinced but went ahead with her plans anyway. Jason was blissfully unaware, and they kept him in the dark.

They drove Mary to the airport the following day. The long flight would be direct to Amsterdam. They walked her as far as the security gate, and then went to a chain store coffee shop for a cup of coffee and a donut. Neither of them had been eating much; Marion left half of her donut on her napkin. They watched Mary's flight take off, and then drove back home. The emptiness of their house was not new but had never felt quite as profound. Marion turned on the television, and Gil picked up a book he had been reading.

The phone rang.

"Should I answer it?" Gil asked.

"No, just unplug the goddamned thing," Marion said. "I'm sick of it."

Gil picked up the receiver anyway. His face changed and his brow tightened.

"I see," he said.

"Yeah. You asshole," the guy on the line said. "We don't need fuckheads like you and your girlfriend running down our country."

"I don't think we ran anything down."

"Well, I'll run your ass down if you ever step in front of my car."

"Word play! Wow, I see you are very clever," Gil said with a heavy dose of irony. "You must be very conservative. I bet you don't believe in things like abortion?"

"Of course not!"

"It's too bad your parents obviously didn't, either. They missed a golden opportunity to improve the human race."

"What?"

Gil hung up and unplugged the phone.

Marion had listened while she was looking at the channel lineup on TV. "Pissing off a nut job is probably not a good idea."

"I wouldn't worry about it. These guys are harmless assholes," Gil said.

"You know that for a fact?" Gil didn't respond. She was quiet while clicking through the channels with the remote control before landing on a police drama. It was as predictable as it was unbelievable. By the end of the show, a handful of agents working for an obscure U.S. government agency keep terrorists from blowing up Los Angeles with a Soviet-era nuke, and no one is the wiser, and all in forty-four minutes with commercials. The show was in its fifth season, and the writers were hard pressed for new ideas. Marion muted the sound as the TV went into a long commercial break between shows.

"That should help with the general level of paranoia," Gil said.

"Stop being such a snob. It's just a TV show. It's escapism. The news is scary enough."

"Sure. Just when people start taking it seriously, we have a problem. It's fiction, not that it could never ever happen, but it's not very likely."

"Not the point, Gil. It's fantasy. No one takes it seriously." Marion was peeved.

"I'm just saying—"

"I'm not interested in what you're saying." Marion unmuted the TV as another show was coming on. "I want to sit here and watch stupid TV shows until I'm tired enough to fall asleep," she said, and turned up the volume as another episode of the same show started up.

# Chapter 14

Dean Malone was in her office when Vice Provost Gary Sime walked in, knocking on her door as he did so. She hated it when he did that. Ever since he was appointed interim vice provost about a year ago his barely contained ego had managed to expose itself on a regular basis. Rather than making an appointment through her secretary, he always took the short walk across campus to see if she was in. She also couldn't stand people who opened her office door as they knocked without waiting for someone to tell them to come in. It seemed to her to show disrespect. As if his entrance was more important than anything else she could be doing.

"Hello, Gary."

"Hi, Pat. Sorry I came over unannounced."

*No you're not. Otherwise you wouldn't have done it.* "Not a problem," she said, although she had plenty of work to do before the general deans' meeting this afternoon, and a visit from an underworked and overpaid executive was the last thing she needed.

"How's your husband?"

"He's fine."

"And the kids?"

"Just fine, both in high school now."

"Maybe they'll come to Bradbury then?"

"I hope so," Pat said. *With what you pay, there isn't much of a choice.* "So, Gary, what's up?"

"Gil Sykes?"

"What about him?" She'd sort of been expecting this visit with the notoriety of the article that was an undertone in the conservative press. She knew that the trustees were all pretty much in agreement with the current ideas about higher education hysterically trumpeted on the conservative talk show circuit: that professors are part-time workers getting full-time pay, that they're all radical liberals trying to indoctrinate their students, that radical feminists and environmentalists are in some kind of conspiracy to take over the world. Pure nonsense. Pat wondered if Gary believed some of it—or maybe all of it.

"I've just talked with Libby Frank"

"Who?"

"The attorney?" he said as if she should know.

"Which attorney?"

"The one who has the radio show."

"Oh, her." Pat had listened to her once or twice. The radio show persona she presented was obnoxious, opinionated, and confrontational, which probably made her a successful attorney, but not necessarily a good one.

"Her daughter Edith is a student here."

"I think I met her at the last open house. She's really young, petite with multicolored hair?"

"Yes. She's precocious and finished high school early," Gary said.

There was a short silence.

"Libby claims that Edith was sexually molested last fall … by a professor."

"Who?"

"The girl wouldn't say, and nothing her mother did could make her."

"So why choose Gil?"

"She passed out in his class and was hospitalized for stress, actually for an abortion."

"So?"

"Well, maybe it was too much for her to be in his class. And she did take a class with him last fall."

"If he molested her, then why the hell would she sign up for another class with him?"

"Maybe he forced her?" Gary postulated. "Maybe he forced her into taking his class?"

Pat burst out laughing. "Sorry." She said between gasps. "Gil would never encourage a student to take a class with him, any student. Believe me. I usually have the opposite problem, convincing students to stay in his classes."

"Is he a bad teacher?"

"The opposite," Pat stopped laughing, and replied coldly, "He expects a lot from his students, and there are much easier options for someone to get Gen Ed credit than taking one of his classes. Maybe she likes him as a teacher? If she's really smart, she might have liked the challenge. Goodness knows we lose enough bright students to other schools because they find no challenge here."

Gary's eyes seemed to lose focus for a moment, as if she'd said something unsayable but also common knowledge. It was clear he didn't like what she said, although he wasn't so indoctrinated in the school public relations to not know that it was true.

"Well, Libby is convinced that Gil had something to do with it."

"Libby?"

"Mrs. Frank."

"Well, I can say with absolute certainty that she's wrong. I've known

Gil for a long time. He wouldn't do something like that."

"We can all be fooled by other people."

"Not in this case. He simply wouldn't." Her voice rose. Gary was beginning to make her angry, something she could usually mask when dealing with his simpering cupidity, but not this time.

"You have strong loyalty to your staff, but in this case, we need to report it to the Title IX coordinator."

"It's total hearsay and speculation. If the girl won't say who it is, won't even file a complaint, we can't assume anything. I'm loyal to my staff because they work hard for us, something you might think about."

"We're not here to discuss that," he said quickly.

"You're the one who mentioned it." She shrugged, and turned her attention to something on her desk, signaling to Gary that she was finished with the conversation. He wasn't.

"That's not the point," he said. "We need to do something about Gil Sykes."

"Why?"

"Sexual harassment can't be ignored," he said firmly.

Pat almost choked on her laughter at the statement from the man who'd been accused for years of making inappropriate sexual remarks to young male coworkers but had never faced any repercussions because he'd always been cunning enough to make sure that no one else was in earshot when he made inappropriate comments.

"No one is saying that it should be. In fact, I've gone on record saying we need to be more aggressive about this. Enabling serial harassers the way we have in the past is a very bad idea, if only that we've now been caught on at least two occasions, and we both know there are a lot more," she paused, and picked up a stack of papers and moved them to the corner of her desk. "However, we need to make sure before we accuse anyone. If we accuse Gil and it's not true, then we've poisoned the well. He'll never get his reputation back. Hell, he might even sue us." Her last remark got his attention, as if the concept of legal action was something that hadn't been discussed at higher levels.

"Well, it's done anyway."

"What is?" she asked.

"The Title IX coordinator has already been informed."

"Then why are you here?"

"To let you know."

"Gee, thanks. Anything else I need to know? Did you outright fire everyone who works for me?"

"Now, Pat," he said in an oily, conciliatory tone, "we have to move forward with this. If it got out in the papers that we had a case of sexual harassment and did nothing about it, they would raise hell."

"You sure it has nothing to do with the fact that the article he worked on with Valerie Dymond is making waves in the conservative community and maybe pissing off some of our more conventional donors?"

He knew she was referring to the fact that one of their alumni had started his own evangelical mega-church and was a multimillionaire who could be very generous with the college when he wanted something. He'd made a lavish donation when his nephew failed out for the third time from his "special program." The boy was allowed back in for a fourth try but had gotten busted for felony possession of narcotics the summer before he started.

"Now, punishing someone for writing an article would be encroaching on academic freedom," Gary said. "We'd never do that."

"Of course not," she said smiling at him. *Do you think I'm really that stupid? Do you think anyone is that stupid?*

***

Gary Sime presided over the meeting. It was well known that he'd been appointed interim vice provost even though several junior level executives had been there far longer than he because the higher ups knew he could be counted on to get committees to vote the "right" way. And it was common knowledge that Bradbury liked to keep people on as "interim" so that they wouldn't have to pay them too much and to keep them on their toes, so, in a pinch, they could be counted on to "do the right thing." Today could go a long way to getting him promoted to "permanent;" he could officially become *one of them* — at least that's what he was led to believe.

Gary called the small group to order. Pat Malone was there, along with Millie Cavanaugh as a representative of the security task force, and Jamie Brit, head of Human Resources. Gary told them briefly what they were there for and read the alleged violations.

"So the complaint does not name any one in particular?" Pat asked.

"No," Jamie answered.

Gary made a face.

"I still think we need to proceed," Millie said.

"To do what?" Pat asked. "We have an alleged seduction of an underage student reported by her parent, not even her, with no teacher named as the abuser."

"Well, it seems to be obvious," Gary said.

"What's obvious?" Pat looked at him directly.

"Well, she passed out in Gil's class," he answered.

"So?" Pat replied. "I've had students vomit in my class because they had the flu. I had one have an epileptic seizure because she forgot to take her medication. Those things had nothing to do with me as a teacher. It's my understanding that Ms. Frank hadn't eaten for two days, nor had she slept, and it was also unofficially mentioned that she'd had an abortion that morning." She let that information be processed for a moment. "As long as we're working on hearsay, I just thought I'd throw that into the mix."

"She could have passed out because of anxiety about going to Gil's class," Millie volunteered, sounding hopeful. Gary nodded in agreement.

"That's another problem I have. If he harassed her, then why would she take another class with him? She signed up, right? No one forced her. There were plenty of other ways for her to fulfill her humanities core requirement."

"Maybe she was intimidated by him?" Millie said.

"And maybe he didn't touch her? We have no evidence it was him. She took six courses last fall, five classes and one overload, with six different teachers, and three graduate teaching assistants. It could even be a teacher that she didn't take a course with, for God's sake." Pat threw up her hands in disgust. "I don't get it. Suddenly we want to railroad this one guy after we've let actual evidence of real harassment go unpunished? Sexual harassment should never be tolerated, but it shouldn't be trivialized, either—or used as a club to beat people up because you don't like what they wrote."

There was a long silence. Gary studied the tabletop in front of him. Millie was interested in something that was out the window.

"I think Pat has a good point," Jamie said, throwing out a lifeline. "We only have a hearsay complaint without anyone named, and it's my understanding that Ms. Frank refuses to name the assailant. It would be rash of us at best to determine it was Professor Sykes, let alone leave us open for a civil action if we're proved wrong."

Her last sentence snapped Gary to attention. There were already two high profile sexual harassment lawsuits leveled at the college from victims whose cases had been swept under the carpet, and he certainly wasn't going to leave them vulnerable to a third.

"Okay. I can talk to Libby Frank again and see if Edith is more cooperative. Until then, maybe we should remove her from the class?" Gary said.

"I think that's a good idea," Millie chimed in. It was clear that she also had serious ambitions for an executive appointment, and her ability to kiss ass was legendary, but Pat noticed she seemed especially keen here to railroad Gil.

"I don't," Pat said. "I suggest we do *nothing at all* until we have some evidence." She looked at them each in turn. "I suggest we table this until we get more proof. We're talking about someone who has been here for a long time without a single incident of this nature."

"That we know of," Gary said.

"Right," Millie said in support. "Who knows what he could have been up to all these years?"

"You're kidding? Right?" Pat said. "Maybe you could ask him if he's stopped beating his wife while you're at it. Or maybe we'll find that he's been whispering obscenities to male colleagues when no one else could hear?"

There was a long silence. Gary turned pink, and a small bead of sweat formed on his forehead. The others were silent. Jamie smiled a little. She liked Gary even less than Pat did.

"Now, Pat, I know he's a friend of yours," Gary said, condescension dripping from his voice.

"No, Gary. He's a professional colleague of mine who has done his job here exceptionally well, and I think he has earned the benefit of the doubt." *You simpering ass,* she added in her head.

"I think the best course of action is to go back to the student and see if she will give us more information. If we make a hasty decision now, it could backfire on us," Jamie said.

"Okay, if that's the way you want it," Gary said. He was smart enough to not leave Bradbury open to another lawsuit, but clever enough to make the decision to not humiliate Gil look like someone else's idea.

"I still think we should pull her out of his class," Millie added, trying to score points with Gary.

"What would be the reason?" Pat asked. *Besides the fact that you don't like him because he calls you on your bullshit.* Millie didn't answer, but again, Pat wondered why the excessive eagerness; Millie usually managed to restrain herself. It was as if she wanted to have Gil charged regardless of the evidence.

"So let's table this for now pending further investigation," Gary said. "Meeting adjourned."

# Chapter 15

Mary Sykes got off her plane at Schiphol Airport. It took a little time to get through customs, but after her passport was stamped, she made her way quickly to the baggage claim. She decided to take a cab to the school, as she needed to check in this afternoon with student services in order to get her room, and the bus would take too long. She'd been very lucky to get the room and knew that it was because of the fact that she had a job with the school.

The airport was the size of a small city, and it took some time to get out and pointed towards Amsterdam. Her phone chimed. It was a text from Paul. She was surprised how much she missed him, but, as they'd both predicted, he was accepted to a program at the University of Virginia, and she was going to be at the University of Amsterdam for at least one year of work and possibly two years of school, so the temporary nature of their relationship had worked out for the best. He'd sent a simple note asking about her travel, and she sent a quick reply. She had discussed her parent's issues with Paul. One moment she thought that her dad might get fired, and the next she thought some right-wing whacko would be gunning him down in his office. She resisted the urge to call her mom.

Mary found her room to be what a New York real estate agent would call "charming." It was simple and tiny, with a bed, desk, dresser, and a small closet. There was a bright white tiled bathroom with a shower, a tiny kitchenette, and a refrigerator that was smaller than what most American students had in their dorm rooms. Her guide spoke to her in English, and Mary practiced her Dutch. She had a couple of weeks of orientation before she would start teaching her intensive English class to students who had come here to do graduate work in psychology but needed some brushing up with English skills. Mary opened her suitcase and started unpacking.

Her parents had offered to buy her new luggage, but she had insisted that her old suitcases were fine, although overzealous baggage handlers and a long stay out in the pouring rain at JFK had left them looking pretty tattered. She thought it made her look like an experienced seasoned traveler, even though most of her travels had been between New York and California. Her phone chimed again: her brother Jason. She had to read the message a few times before it sunk in.

*Dad 2B on ptrick henri show b4 book comes out*
She couldn't believe it. She texted back, *WTF???*
His response was a shrug emoticon.

# Chapter 16

*Two weeks prior.*

Millie Cavanaugh was on bottom, which was unusual for her; Peter Morton was on top thrusting for all he was worth, like a jackrabbit. What he lacked in experience he made up for in enthusiasm. Millie had already climaxed and was hoping that Peter would soon. He always took too long. She idly wondered if he'd gotten his technique from streaming too many porno videos.

They'd had a satisfying long weekend at a rented room with a kitchenette near the beach, far from Bradbury, but now she was a little sore and chafed, and starting to get bored with her new boy toy. She pushed him to the side after he finished, and then rolled out of bed, put on a white cotton robe and headed for the bathroom. It was early afternoon; they would need to leave tomorrow morning for the four-hour drive back. Almost all of the cabins were vacant since it was too cold to swim and too windy to hang out on the beach. A young couple was attempting to sit on beach chairs, but the whipping stinging sand drove them back into their cabin. Millie watched them through the blinds. Powerful waves smashed on the sand, churning up brown seaweed. She poured some wine and sipped it; there was a randy smell in the room. She turned to see Peter asleep on the bed, a sheet covering his loins like Christ in a Pieta.

They had met at one of those interminable faculty mixers that always happened around midterm. She'd been drinking too much wine and hadn't eaten. Peter noticed she had staggered off in the direction of the parking lot, and knew she was too intoxicated to drive, so he offered her a ride home. She took it. Peter was very handsome, and she was intrigued, having previously encountered him in the hallways a few times when she had to speak with Gil on committee business. Since Peter, who was Gil's TA, was a humanities graduate student, he would never take a course with her because she taught in the business program. His scope of study had narrowed to one field and one department in that field, with perhaps one or two professors who were experts.

Peter had been a gentleman and had brought her home that night. What happened next was entirely her idea. She invited him in for a cup of coffee, but before it was done brewing she had grabbed him and kissed him, pulling off his shirt to reveal his very buff torso with a tattoo of blue and black geometric lines that went across his chest and all the way around to his back. She had stripped him almost naked in her kitchen and thought of having sex on the granite countertop but decided the bed would be far more comfortable.

The coffee maker had finished filling the pot, the timer had shut off the hotplate, and the coffee was room temperature before they came back downstairs. That had been a few months ago.

Her husband was one of the English Department's well-published stars who, at the time had been gone for three months on a fellowship to London researching his latest book, a biographical critique of Harold Pinter that focused more on his acting than his playwriting.

He had since returned, which was why they were renting a cabin at a seaside hotel way out of season. She had said she was going to a small conference in Buffalo. They actually went in the opposite direction.

She thought for a minute about the man she'd married. They'd met, of course, on campus, and, after a whirlwind courtship, and despite his reputation for serial infidelity, Millie became his third wife.

At first, she had ignored the rumors and turned a blind eye to his disheveled clothes, a blind ear to the inconsistencies in his stories about his whereabouts. The year before, though, he had a notorious and very public fling with a visiting professor from France, making no effort to even pretend to be discreet. Millie had responded by having her own affair with a mutual friend of theirs, but she found it unsatisfying.

Her musings were interrupted by Peter, who was waking up.

"You hungry?" she asked.

"A little. Any food left?"

"No, we'll have to go to the store or find a restaurant."

"Okay." He started to get dressed, and as he covered himself slowly with clothes, finding most of them in a pile on the floor, she regretted having mentioned food, even though she hadn't eaten since that morning when she used the last of the eggs for omelets. They drove about a mile up the road to a popular restaurant. The smell of fried seafood hung in the air outside, and even at the late hour for lunch, there were cars in the parking lot. The restaurant had a tacky sea motif with ropes and buoys and other nautical tackle hanging from the walls and ceiling. They ordered and sat quietly looking at the walls.

"Arrgh, this place makes me want to talk like a pirate," Peter said.

"Don't," Millie replied.

"Sorry."

"How is Gil Sykes this semester? Nutty as usual?"

"He's not so bad. He's going to be my thesis chairman," Peter said.

"Really?" She sipped her soda. "Might not be a great idea. He can be a real prick when he wants to."

"I know. But I want to write on the American Romantics and he's the only one on staff who really knows anything about them." He gave her a lopsided grin. "It's either him or your husband, and I don't think that would be a good idea."

"No. It. Would. Not," Millie said.

"Thought so."

That was the first time either of them had mentioned her husband directly. Peter hadn't even known she was married when they first slept together. She'd casually mentioned it the next morning when she made a fresh pot of coffee. It had bothered him a little then, but no longer. He found the whole thing somewhat amusing and a little ironic. He had really been attracted to Millie, but figured her to be far beyond his reach, and then to become her lover, so quickly, so effortlessly left him a little bemused.

"Gil isn't so bad. He's actually a pretty good teacher."

"Really? I thought his students hated him."

"Some do. But usually just the ones looking for an easy A." He finished his glass of wine and motioned the waitress for another. "In fact, we've had some pretty good students in the last couple of classes. One actually took two classes with him. She's really bright."

"Really?" she said, not very interested, just trying to hold up her end of the conversation.

"Yeah. Edith Frank. She's bright as hell." Peter was eating so he didn't notice the profound change of expression on Millie's face.

"Really?" she said in a completely different octave than before.

Peter went on eating and talking, oblivious to the change in tone.

"Yeah. She's really petite, pastel hair, always has an armload of books with her, kind of sweet, really." He continued, getting more and more enthusiastic. "In the discussion group, it was usually a conversation between the two of us. No one else really reads the books with any depth of understanding—or at all." He laughed.

Millie listened intently, her eyes focused strictly on him.

"She's really great, smartest kid in any of my classes." He finished his key lime pie and looked across at Millie. "Are you okay? Is your food okay? You look a little funny."

"When did you sleep with her?"

"What?"

"When did you fuck her?" she hissed.

His face tightened, and his eyes twitched in emotion.

"That's not your business. We're not married you know." He added for effect, "At least *I'm* not."

"That's not the point, you idiot." Millie was getting loud enough for other customers to hear, and a few were looking in their direction, "She's only sixteen. She's underage. Her mom knows half the trustees personally. She's been having a total fit."

"It was nothing," Peter said, trying more to convince himself. Not only did he break the rules of his contract forbidding sex with his students, but he'd broken the law. "It was just a simple hook up at a party. Friendly sex. No big deal. She went home. I went home. It was nothing."

"She got pregnant," Millie said to her empty soda glass.

It was Peter's turn to look sick. She regarded him for a moment. "Sorry, Peter. She won't say who it was—so far." She studied the bottom of her glass as if looking for an answer. "She had an abortion. That's why she passed out in class that day at the beginning of the semester." She looked across the table at him. She'd struck the blow she'd wanted. He was pale. His hands were shaking.

He reached for the wine glass in a jerky, spastic motion, and knocked it over so hard it broke and splashed wine all over the tablecloth and all over his face. It looked like blood. An alert waitress ran over with a wet towel. She scooped up the mess by taking up the corners of the tablecloth and carrying away the whole disaster: plates, cups, broken glass, silverware and all as if it was a large cloth bag. She gave the wet towel to Peter to clean himself up.

The naked wooden table with a yellowed high-gloss varnish, pockmarked with dozens of cigarette burns and white ashtray rings from a different epoch, dimly reflected two people: the attractive, but now ashen, young man holding his head in his hands, and the older, sharply attractive woman with deeply cruel eyes.

# Chapter 17

Gil and Valerie were in her office late in the afternoon. Printed pages were spread out on a large table that was under the window. They were going over the manuscript. A major press was going to publish their book. He was now listed as the co-author and had provided all the background material for the chapters on colonial literature. The publisher was hoping that it would be an academic bestseller, which would be about a tenth of the typical New York Times bestseller, but the controversy around the article could push up sales. Gil was marking up some pages that were in his lap while Valerie was bent over the table with a pencil in her hand. She looked up at the clock on her desk, stretched, and put the pencil down.

"I need a break."

"Me, too," Gil said, and sat up in the chair to stretch. "This is a very tight deadline they put us on."

"They want to get the book out while there's interest. At least, that's what they told me," Valerie said. Since she was the primary author, she dealt more with the publisher than Gil.

"I don't think interest is going to flag anytime soon," Gil said, thinking of the fact that Patrick Henri was now beating them up nightly on his show, and Lenny Trout was probably starting to sell his books again, so his criticism was getting even more strident.

They still got a few unwanted phone calls. Most of them were from those who genuinely liked her article. Some were from people who wanted to share a pet bizarre theory, usually involving extraterrestrials, the Deep State, or both. But the third category was the one that was the scariest: people who threatened them.

"I don't like the idea of going on the Patrick Henri show. He's just an ass," Val said. "It was the publisher's idea. They told me that any publicity is good publicity."

"I don't like the idea, either. He can be difficult, and he has a tendency to simply try to beat people over the head with irrelevant facts that are usually wrong rather than actually discuss an issue."

"Yeah." She sighed. "We'll have to be on our toes."

"Yes, and anticipate his moves as best we can. We really should be on the public networks, NPR and PBS."

"That's right, but it could also be the problem?"

"How so?" Gil asked.

"Academics only talk to other academics. It's elitist. Non-academic people feel left out. It makes them suspicious."

"At one time, major philosophers actually were read by the general public. William James, George Santayana, Simone de Beauvoir. They wrote for people outside the ivy tower. They had a point, though, philosophy has to understandable, or no one can follow it. If it's so jargoned up that only a few hundred people in the world know what you're talking about, then what good is it? Maybe you're right. In a way, we did it to ourselves."

"Well, we might have broken the barrier now," she said thoughtfully, walking over to Gil, who was rubbing his neck. She massaged his neck and shoulders with her fingers and heard the crunching sound of a vertebra sliding back into place.

"Wow. Didn't know my neck was that tight. I'll have to make an appointment for a massage," Gil said.

Valerie went back to the table and started to organize the papers, putting them in piles by chapter and placing her notes on top of each pile. "I might put this up until tomorrow. I'm supposed to go out to dinner tonight."

"I don't think I've seen your fiancé for almost a year now. Have you set a date for the wedding?"

"Probably next summer if he gets promoted."

"He works for a software company, right?"

"Yes. Data Systems."

"I've heard of them."

"They grew very fast, but now the whole industry is holding its collective breath because there are too many data management companies, so we'll see what's going to happen. There's been talk of layoffs." She shrugged. "Hell, even I could be looking for work soon."

"No way."

"I wish that were true, but, like most colleges, Chamberlain, is a *very* conservative place. Even if many of the professors are liberal, the executives and trustees who run the place aren't. And some of the trustees really hate my article. I'm sure they'll like the book even less. They also don't like all the vicious craziness in the right-wing press. They always manage to mention that I'm from Chamberlain College."

"But you have tenure."

"Yes. But they can still figure out ways to get rid of me."

"True," Gil said, "but I wouldn't worry about it. You're publishing an important book. Certainly they can see that?"

"Maybe."

Valerie left to meet her fiancé. Gil stayed another hour to finish up the chapter he was editing. Every now and then, he'd get up and stare out the window. Her third-floor office faced the parking lot, and there was a long ramp near the front for handicapped parking that went to three large parking spaces. It was usually empty, or a campus security vehicle was there while the officer walked around the parking lot booting cars or writing tickets. Gil noticed a late model SUV with a handicapped tag hanging from the rearview mirror. It looked to him like someone was sitting in the driver's side, but the angle was too sharp for him to really see much. As he watched, the vehicle started up and drove slowly away. Gil went back to work, finished the chapter, and went home.

Marion wasn't there to greet him. There was no note on the table. She had said that morning that she was going to be busy with some family business. There was plenty in the fridge that he could heat up for dinner. After changing his clothes, he heated up some leftovers for supper, turned on the TV and listened to the news until his food was warm, then set up the TV tray and watched the rest of the news.

***

Marion left the Planned Parenthood clinic with her niece, the one who had gotten married the year before. She and her husband were both still in college and had no money or insurance to see a doctor. The niece's car had broken down, which made matters even worse, and she had called her favorite aunt, sounding desperate. She hadn't dared call her very religious mother, the one who had insisted that she never get married in the first place since her husband was from a different faith. Actually, he had no faith in particular. So Marion had given her a ride to the clinic for a gynecological exam, and for her to get a prescription for birth control pills. The doctor had given her a month's worth of samples, but Marion drove her to the pharmacy and paid for a full three months prescription of the pills. This was no time for her and her husband to start a family. Then they stopped at the supermarket, and Marion bought her some groceries while she shopped for herself and Gil. Her niece was grateful and couldn't thank her aunt Marion enough when she dropped her off at her apartment.

Gil had finished his supper, and was watching the end of the newscast when he heard Marion pull up, so he went back to the kitchen to make up a plate for her, and then went out to the driveway to help carry in the few bags she'd left in the car. He noticed what looked like the same SUV from earlier in the afternoon parked across the street and up the block. Gil left the bags in the car and walked toward it. The driver started the vehicle and drove off, driving by the house, looking the other way as he passed so Gil couldn't see his face.

"What's up?" Marion asked.

"Not sure," Gil said. "I saw a vehicle this afternoon in the parking lot in front of Val's office, and I think it was the same one here. Did anyone follow you home? He wasn't there when I got here."

"No, but I wasn't looking for anyone, so I can't be sure," she said. "Kind of creepy, don't you think?"

"Yeah. Well, let's not worry about it. Might be nothing at all," he said and picked up the bags from the trunk of her car.

"At least the phone calls have tapered off. We're down to about one or two death threats a day," Marion said.

He looked down the road where the SUV had gone.

"Yeah. Let's not look for more trouble."

# Chapter 18

Gil and Valerie got out of the limo at Rockefeller Center. A young man met them and took them to the elevator and up to the Patrick Henri studio. A makeup artist quickly went over each of them, and they waited in the Green Room for the show to start. It would actually air later the next day.

Patrick Henri was in his own dressing room. Attendants were swarming around him applying makeup, adjusting his microphone, which was always turned up much louder than his guests, and getting him ready for taping the show. He patted the new intern on the butt as she turned to go. She froze for a minute, shook her head, and kept walking. She knew he could destroy her career, or at least make sure she failed her internship and had to repeat her senior year in college. He'd certainly done it before, and was known for getting even with women who refused him. She shook it off and moved on.

His director, John Bentley, arrived. The two men had been friends for years. They'd met when on assignment for a cable news outfit, covering a coup that had cropped up in North Africa. They never even made it to the country. Patrick Henri and his newfound buddy John rented a hotel room in Cairo, and mostly made up the stuff they sent back, getting a translator to give them the details from the local Arabic television station that was reporting on the coup, and grabbing a picture off the TV in their room with a digital camera to send along with the stories. With their shared opinion of what constituted responsible journalism, they became lifelong friends, and Patrick had brought John along when he had found his successful formula of anti-intellectualism, xenophobia, coupled with a dash of outright racism that played to the worst characteristics of the American personality and made him a millionaire TV personality impersonating a journalist.

He and Bentley cleared the dressing room and planned out the finer points of the show that they were about to start recording. Like all of his shows, Henri had at least one unpleasant surprise ready for his guests that was guaranteed to get his ratings back up to justify his salary.

"Just remember to lay into the guy. Thank goodness he's white. You don't want to come across as racist—or sexist—so leave the woman alone," Bentley said. Patrick had crossed the line more than once and had lost sponsors because of outright racist comments.

Patrick Henri did his intro and monologue, and while the show was in its first commercial break, Gil and Valerie were seated next to him. Gil was surprised at how small the set really was, and how packed the whole studio seemed to be with equipment, lights, cameras, and people running around getting last-minute items in place. One sound technician fiddled with Valerie's microphone almost until the time came to roll the cameras. Her soft voice was barely registering on the equipment. He ducked away just as the director called for action.

Patrick Henri looked bright orange under the lights, and began with introducing the two of them, mispronouncing the name of Valerie's college.

"So," he said, turning to her, "you claim that Thomas Jefferson is a phony?"

"No," Valerie said, "I just found evidence when I was working on sabbatical in Haiti that some of his ideas could have come from another source."

"So you're just saying that he's a thief?"

"You're a little out of context. She said no such thing" Gil said. "What we've found is simply that the wording of a French privateer called Jean the Mulatto, or Black Caesar, who had made a Charter with his crew, was very similar to some passages in the Declaration of Independence."

"So you're saying Jefferson stole his ideas from a black pirate?" Patrick Henri said with his trademark sarcasm, including his arrogant smirk. The audience groaned on cue.

"Not really, but our book goes into much more detail, and is an analysis of the colonial period. Jean actually became a successful businessman in Haiti. There was a rich mixture of cultures and ideas all through the Americas long before the Revolution," Valerie said, trying to be clear, but Patrick Henri used it to jump on one of his favorite hobbyhorses.

"You mean *multiculturalism*?" He spat the word out like he was talking about a venereal disease. His audience booed.

"Yes," she said, being hopeful and maybe a little naïve, as if she were explaining to a student who had asked a legitimate question. "There were French, Portuguese, Spanish, Dutch, and English colonies in the New World, along with native peoples and West African slaves. It was the original multicultural zone, especially in the Caribbean where native people and Europeans made first contact—" She was going to be more explicit when he smiled tolerantly at her and cut her off to go to commercial.

Makeup artists and technicians touched up the three of them, adjusting and fine-tuning, and then they had about a minute before the director called for action.

"We are with two academics who are trying to prove that Thomas

Jefferson, one of our founding fathers, was a liar and a thief," Patrick Henri said by way of re-introduction.

"My goodness, man, have you even been listening to us? That's not what we contend at all," Gil said. "what we were saying in our book is that—"

He couldn't finish because Patrick Henri interrupted him and mentioned the criticism of their book by Lenny Trout. Gil was surprised that Patrick Henri, or more likely, one of his interns, had even heard of him.

"Professor Trout simply pointed out something we admitted in both the article and in our forthcoming book," Valerie said.

"You mean that you made the whole thing up?" Patrick said, rolling his eyes to his audience, who laughed as they were supposed to.

"No." Valerie kept cool. Gil wanted to punch him. She said, "We simply offer up the facts and show some logical conclusions. There are an awful lot of coincidences, for instance the young daughter of the first mate was a slave at Tuckahoe plantation when Jefferson was a teenager, and—"

"But there is no proof that they even knew each other."

"He had a history of—"

"Not that Sally Hemings baloney again!" Patrick Henri turned beet red and quivering with indignation, something he was well known for, and could do at will, along with shedding plenty of indignant patriotic tears. "You two are an example of what's wrong with this country. You liberal elitists want to tear down everything we stand for."

"If getting to the truth is wrong, then so be it. We investigate and go where the facts lead us. Unless of course, you prefer to choose ignorance," Gil said, but was almost drowned out by the enraged audience. Of course, Patrick Henri knew exactly which audience buttons to push, and he also knew enough to cut to commercial when the other person made a good point, which was what he did.

The three made a study of how not to look at each other during the short break, and then as the cameras started up again, Patrick Henri seemed to change tone, and sounded almost friendly, which was, as they knew, when he was the most poisonous.

"You have a nephew named Richard?"

"Yes," Gil said frowning. "I *had* a nephew; he passed away late last year."

"You have my condolences," he said insincerely. "You got him in school at Bradbury?"

"I asked that he be admitted."

"Come now, Professor, you're too modest. He never would have made it in with his high school grades."

"Perhaps."

"Did you pull a few strings to get him in?"

"That has nothing to do with this conversation."

"Isn't it true that you recommended that a felon be admitted to your school?" His line of inquiry shifted.

"No."

"Wasn't he charged with a felony when he went to Bradbury? Isn't it true that he caused a serious accident and almost killed another person?"

"He was charged with felony DWI at the end of the one semester he was there. Not that it makes any difference. We are here to discuss the book, not my nephew."

"Of course, it makes no difference if he's a felon or not since he's dead anyway. Of course, I wouldn't want my kids going to school with a felon."

Patrick Henri then switched gears and asked, "How long have you two been working on this project together?"

"I don't know. About a year now, right, Gil?" Valerie said.

"Yes. Valerie started the research, and then asked me to help her out since this time period was more my area of expertise."

"So you two have spent a lot of time together?"

"Really?" Valerie said a question at the end. A photo appeared on the screen of Valerie massaging Gil's shoulders while in her office working on the proofs. It was grainy and taken from a distance.

"Looks like you two are working really hard here," Patrick Henri said, smirking and rolling his eyes; his audience laughed.

"Deceptive," Gil yelled. "We had been editing the book for hours."

"Did I say anything?" Patrick Henri pleaded, his eyes wide with false innocence. "By the way, here's another interesting picture." A photo of Marion walking out of a Planned Parenthood Clinic with their niece appeared on the monitor. "What are your wife and daughter doing leaving an abortion clinic?"

"That's not our daughter, that's our niece," Gil said, his voice rising a few decibels. "And I have no idea what they're doing. My guess is getting a checkup? Where did you get these photographs?"

"They were legally obtained."

"Bull!" Gil said.

"Why, professor, please watch your language," Patrick Henri said in mock offense. He let the photo of Marion in front of the clinic, where the sign for Planned Parenthood had been heavily enhanced so that it was almost glowing, linger on the screen a few more seconds. "Not only that, but I have an avadavat signed by a hotel housekeeper in Chicago where she states under oath that she saw you two together in the tenth-floor hallway going to Val's room." The paper replaced the photo on screen.

"Of course we were together. We presented a paper together," Valerie said.

But it was far too late for anything as delicate and fragile as the truth to prevail. Patrick Henri did his trademark eye roll one more time, and his audience roared as he wrapped up the show and cut to the final commercial.

Later in the limo heading back home Gil and Valerie sat in silence, and then Gil spoke up. "Well, at least I know one good thing."

"What's that?"

"The guy in the big black SUV wasn't trying to kill me. He just wanted to get a few pictures for his boss."

# Chapter 19

Millie walked into Gary Sime's office while knocking on the door, ignoring his secretary, who told her she'd have to wait until she paged Gary because he was on the phone. Gary hung up soon after she entered.

"How's everything, Millie?"

"Fine, Gary."

"You want to see me?"

"I certainly do." She sat down in a chair across from him and pulled out a letter. "I received this from one of the graduate student assistants." She handed it to Gary. He read it, slowly, pausing with his eyebrows up over the main point.

"This is anonymous, though," he said, while scanning the letter for a name or signature

"Let's just say the student is worried about retaliation. He's in a delicate position," Millie said.

Gary smiled; he was fully aware of Peter and his *delicate* position. Millie's latest sexual liaison was already old news, not even part of the usual lunchtime gossip anymore. He also knew that Peter was Gil's teaching assistant, and that he would be the perfect person to accuse him if it went to the next level, although the letter mentioned only a senior member of the faculty, no name. Gary was only too happy to bring the letter to the attention of the trustees, and especially to Libby Frank. It was not enough evidence to bring Gil—or anyone—up on charges, but certainly enough to suspend him pending investigation, maybe even force him into retirement. In any case, he'd make sure that investigation took a long, long time.

After the Patrick Henri Show, the more conservative members of the board, which was most of them, who had already been putting a lot of pressure on the administration to find a reason to get rid of Gil, redoubled their efforts, especially when it came out about his nephew being a student there. The college president, however, would have nothing to do with pushing Gil out of his job, and had given them a flat no. But the president was getting ready to retire, and Gary was nothing if not ambitious. The idea of moving up to the president's seat had been his goal from the start.

Gil was in his office getting ready for class when Gary knocked on his door. He was with Jamie Britt, head of Human Resources. Three people in the small space made if uncomfortably crowded. Gil placed the book he was reading on the desk. Gary wormed his way over to the only chair and sat down. Jamie remained standing.

"I can get you a folding chair," Gil said.

"That won't be necessary," Jamie replied.

"So what's up?"

"I have a letter that makes some strong allegations against you, Gil," Jamie said. "Gary gave it to me."

"Sounds serious." Gil sat up straighter.

"It claims that you had relations with one of your students, Edith Frank."

There was a long pause.

"That's absolutely ridiculous. Who said such a thing? My God, the girl's younger than my kids."

Jamie showed him a copy of the letter.

"It's not signed? It doesn't even name me directly?" Gil said. "You're bothering me about this, and it's not even signed?"

"Title IX allows for anonymous reporting."

"It also assumes that you can use your discretion and common sense, that you would know better than act on one report that doesn't even name anyone."

"It's a board of trustees' thing." Gary spoke up. "We got beaten up because of the last couple of times we didn't act, so now they're overreacting." He shrugged in sympathy. "I wish there was something I could do."

"Bullshit, Gary. Don't expect me to play your game. This has your hand all over it. You started out as a sycophant and a toady doing the trustees' dirty work, and you keep after it, for what? Is your integrity worth a pat on the head? Everyone knows the reason that the other sexual abuse cases went off the reservation is the fact that those very same trustees tried to systematically shut them down, and two of them backfired, one because the girl was a little too naïve to keep it to herself, and the other because the basketball coach's rant and rave went viral all over the internet and was made into a meme, and we were made a laughingstock."

"We've made arrangements for your teaching assistant to take your classes. You will have to leave pending an investigation, but we will keep it quiet," Gary went on, as if this, too, were his idea. "No need for anyone to go to the press."

Gil looked at Jamie, "You go along with this?" he asked.

She looked down and then out the window of his office. "Right now, I don't a have a lot of choice," she said.

"Does Pat Malone know what you two are up to?" Gil asked.

Both were very quiet.

"Of course she doesn't," Gil said. "Neither of you would have the guts to run this by her."

"Gil," Jamie said, quietly, "we *will* investigate. I'm sure you'll be cleared. It's not like—"

"Yes, and you'll take all the poison out of the well, too? You know damn well after this that there will always be a lingering doubt." He paused and looked at Jamie. "I know this is not your doing, Jamie."

"We had no choice. We had to act on the letter," Gary said.

"One anonymous letter? Nothing else?" Gil was incredulous. He sighed. "Well, if it was good enough for Joe Stalin, it's good enough for Bradbury College."

"Now, Gil, if I had a choice," Gary said, deeply patronizing.

"Stop treating me as if I'm stupid, Gary. Save it for someone who has to pretend to believe your drivel. Your stink is all over this. You've been a simpering low-life duplicitous mendacious ass since you got here. And it would be exactly your idea to use a bogus charge of sexual harassment as a way to curry favor with the trustees. I hope they give you a nice reward. Who knows, maybe they'll let *you* win at golf for a change?" Gil spoke without raising his voice.

Gary looked as stunned as if Gil had shouted at him; few managed to tell him the truth to his face.

Jamie held her hand over her mouth so Gary couldn't see that she was smiling.

the papers. There'll be an investigation I'm sure. But Sykes still gets paid. Do I make myself clear? The man draws his pay until this thing is settled. I still don't believe a word of this nonsense. And if Millie leaked this to the press, I will make sure that all the rumors about her are treated with the same vigilance and interest that she seems to be taking in Gil's private life. Does she think for one minute that no one notices her continual affairs, not to mention that randy husband of hers? We haven't dismissed anyone on moral grounds for a very long time, but it can still be done." He looked at Gary, "We're done here."

***

Dr. Bill showed up for his appointment a little early. Christina had a small waiting room, just a chair and a table with a few odd magazines. He sat down and leafed through a magazine about the Hudson Valley while he waited. His back was throbbing with the deep pain from arthritis, but he was trying hard not to take any of the prescribed medication because one of the drugs was bad for his stomach, and the other made him sleepy and dizzy. Christina worked wonders for him, but sometimes his busy schedule made it impossible for him to schedule the bi-monthly appointments he needed to manage his pain.

When she was ready for him, he went in and positioned himself on the massage table, face down, his head in the padded hole. She began working on his lower back.

"Have you been doing the exercises I suggested?"

"Uh-huh," he replied.

She worked on his back in silence. Usually he was quiet, and she took her cue from that. His back was like a rock and he winced when she touched him, so she decided to start with some ultrasound.

"I'm going to try to use the ultrasound to loosen you up. You're very tight today." She hooked up the pads and turned on the machine, set the intensity, and set the timer.

"Work," Dr. Bill said, the word muffled by the table.

"There does seem to be a lot going on all of the sudden. I know that Gary's been busy," she said.

He remained silent for a bit, and then said, "It's just that damn business with Gil. For goodness' sakes I will never believe that the man would be so stupid he'd have an affair with one of his students, let alone one that young. I just can't believe it."

"I agree," she said. "I've known him and Marion for years."

The timer beeped, and she took off the electrodes and began to work on his lower back again.

"It's that article, too, that he wrote with that professor from

Chamberlain, the one about Thomas Jefferson. It has everyone riled up. It's not my field, and I don't really care, but some of the board members are upset about it. They probably never read it." He grunted as she continued the massage. "It would have gone away, but now this issue makes it front page again, not to mention the terrorist thing. And the college is mentioned every time."

As he talked, she could feel his back tense up.

"Maybe you shouldn't think about it right now?"

"You're right," he agreed. "One thing, though, I still can't figure out how that reporter, Sasha Korbet, got all that information. No one's supposed to be talking to the press. No one. Period."

It was Christina's turn to tense up, remembering the call that Gary had received that day. Her fingers gently worked Dr. Bill's back, as she expertly loosened the muscles and improved his circulation. She knew, of course, that his pain was really caused by arthritis that was between the vertebrae of his lower back, damaging the cartilage between the vertebrae, which would eventually disappear until the bones touched each other. His back was badly inflamed, so she knew there was a limit to what she could do.

"You might try some ginger tea when you get home and maybe put some hops in it if you have any. You can get them loose at the health food store on Main Street, the place next to the hardware store. They sell them in bulk in the back of the store. Your lower back is very inflamed, but I'm not telling you anything you don't know. Be sure to keep exercising. You've got to keep the blood circulation in that area."

She'd found it best to not let the patient know when she knew he wasn't quite being honest with her. She knew that Dr. Bill would get back to the gym when he had the chance. "And I know you don't like to take them, but if it gets any worse, you should take your anti-inflammatory and pain pills. Don't wait until you can't move. You need to get out in front of this."

Christina was torn. She liked Dr. Bill, and he'd always treated her with respect, but she was Gary's secretary and had loyalty to him, too, not to mention needing her job.

She left the room so Dr. Bill could get dressed, and in a minute or so he was in her kitchen handing her his credit card. She swiped it with her smartphone and sent the receipt to his email. Then she had an idea, and quickly sent him another email. One with no text at all, just a photo attached—the one she'd taken that morning of Gary's phone showing Sasha Korbet as the caller. His special-order hand-tooled turquoise leather case was unmistakable; anyone who knew Gary would be able to tell it was his phone, and Dr. Bill knew him very well.

# Chapter 25

Marcus looked at the cotton field. He'd been picking since sunrise, and there always seemed to be more white fluffy balls than when he started. He looked behind him to see the row of bare grey stalks, reassuring himself that some progress had been made. He was ahead of all the other pickers, so he took a minute to stretch. He knew not to take too long because that would call unwanted attention. He thought of another form of unwanted attention. Jewel, his daughter who had been born a year after his capture, had grown into a lovely maiden. She was working in the house as a maid with her mother June. He knew that the young cousin of the Master who was known to come for long visits had his eye on her. Everyone knew. It was discussed in oblique, coded language because it was something that wasn't supposed to happen, something that was never mentioned directly, like a bad omen or a dead child. Thomas Jefferson was young but insisted on spending time with Jewel on the pretext of her being his maid.

Marcus continued picking his row. Jefferson was visiting again and planned on staying for the harvest before leaving for William and Mary to study law. Jewel was assigned to clean his room, and it was common knowledge that her "cleaning" lasted late into the night. As it turned out, Jewel stayed in the manor house; they didn't see her for the rest of the week.

Marcus worked until his back would no longer straighten up and the drivers actually had to force him to go home to his shack. June had long since been there and had left him some supper on the table, covered with a tin pot so the flies wouldn't land all over it, before she'd gone back to work. Since the Master was entertaining guests at the main house, she'd be late getting home. Marcus picked at the black-eyed peas and fatback dripping with lard and nibbled on the piece of cornbread that covered the entire plate. June always made the cornbread with plenty of molasses, so it was light brown instead of yellow. Eventually, he finished and went to bed. Too tired to think, too tired to stay awake, Marcus slept and dreamed of turquoise blue water, and he dreamed of Jean.

\*\*\*

Jefferson was thinking about his studies at William and Mary. This school year he would graduate, and he was excited about the prospect of becoming a lawyer. The carriage was taking him away from his cousin's plantation. He would have preferred riding a horse to Williamsburg, but his cousin had insisted on lending him his carriage and horses, claiming he wanted Thomas to be fresh for the first days of school. After his studies, Jefferson would have to practice law with an established attorney before being admitted to the bar, so it would be a long time before he would be able to return. He sat in the two-wheeled carriage driven by one of his cousin's slaves reading a book on architecture that he'd just purchased before coming to Tuckahoe, a practice that he would continue his whole life, ultimately building one of the largest private libraries in North America, but his thoughts kept slipping to the other document he carried. He'd been astonished when Jewel had shown it to him a couple of nights earlier. She'd said her father had given it to her.

He unrolled it again, as he'd had done repeatedly over the past few days. It had been the Charter of a French Privateer from the last war. Jewel had told him her father was the captain of the ship, but Jefferson instantly dismissed that as impossible. How could a Negro be the captain of a ship? Even a pirate ship. They simply didn't have the native intelligence. It was utter nonsense.

He opened the vellum roll and read the words *Tous Les Hommes Naissent Égaux*. A chill went through him. Part of him understood the fundamental truth of those words, and part of him promptly rejected it. He rolled up the document, tied it with the piece of green silk that it had come with, tucked it deep into his coat as if to hide it, and then resumed reading his book.

# Chapter 26

Patrick Henri always left about a minute at the end of his broadcast to address his audience directly so he could summarize or harp on his latest outrage. He looked earnestly into the camera, making sure that it favored his best side, and spoke in his rumbling baritone.

"Friends, fellow patriots, I need to let you know about a recent guest we had on this show a little over a month ago—actually, two guests." He paused for Gil's photo to appear. "It appears that the good professor, Gilbert Sykes, the guy who co-wrote a book accusing Thomas Jefferson of stealing his ideas for this great county from a black pirate, was arrested for sexually harassing one of his students."

The screen shifted to the headline and photo from the local paper of Gil holding Edith Frank. "It seems that our professor friend is simply a common criminal, harassing the young women we put in his care."

Gil's image flashed again, then the camera cut to Patrick Henri. "Just thought you'd want to know. I know I would if I had a kid at Bradbury College." Managing to look shocked, he added, "Oh, and the real kicker is that my sources say the kid's just turned sixteen."

He gave his audience a minute to absorb what he'd said, then, as if it had just occurred to him, said, "Oh, yeah, that woman who was with him, Professor Valerie Dymond, the other author? Well, she got fired for mishandling thousands in grant money. Why am I not surprised? Her kind is so used to handouts. Makes you wonder how she and her boyfriend spent it. It must have been a real good time, if you know what I mean!" His face lit up in a leer, the audience cheered, and then the show cut to commercial as the closing music cued up.

Patrick Henri took out his earpiece and stood. He felt pretty good about that one, even though the lawyers had insisted that he say that the man was only charged with the crime, and not necessarily guilty. There would be a quick disclaimer mixed in with the rolling credits, that a viewer, watching closely and able to speed read, might be able to see.

A few people congratulated him on the show, and he nodded to them as he went to his dressing room. He started to remove his makeup and checked to see if he had a Viagra handy, then he used the intercom to buzz his good friend Bentley.

"Send in one of the interns. I need to have someone take a few notes for next week's show before I forget."

"Okay, anyone in particular?"

"That blonde. You know, the one from NYU?"

"Okay, Pat."

Patrick Henri took a blue pill and waited for the intern.

***

Gil and Marion got out of their car and surveyed the damage that was still noticeable in the siding above the new garage door. Their homeowner's insurance company had replaced the door but was giving them a hard time about the melted siding. Gil's old car had been towed away right after the adjuster had shown up. As Gil had anticipated, they wouldn't pay him anything for it. It was too old for comprehensive insurance, and it had been destroyed in a terrorist act, so he was out of luck.

Marion opened the door and Gil dragged in their suitcases. After they'd heard from Officer Kohl, they'd decided to remain at the vacation rental for the rest of the two-week stay they'd booked and spent the time relaxing and staying off the internet and social media sites.

A short while later, when the police officers knocked on their door, neither had any idea why they might be there. Gil thought it could be a follow up to the thwarted bombing. He was astonished when one officer read him his rights and took him to the station to book him on charges of sexual harassment of a minor.

Lance Hendricks had been the District Attorney for three terms now and had been reasonably competent, but relatively undistinguished as a prosecutor or as a legal administrator. People could say that "he didn't offend anyone," and he was elected on the strength of that attribute and his family name. Lance was distantly related to Colonel Sam Hendricks who'd raised a local militia and relieved General Washington at a particularly difficult battle that had gone very badly for the rebels; in fact, they were facing utter defeat. The Colonel's reinforcements held the British at bay, and then forced them back to their ships in the Hudson.

After the war, a grateful nation gave the Colonel a very large piece of property right on the Hudson River that had eventually become the small city that housed Bradbury College.

Lance had been to the riverfront that morning, a place he found he needed to go when he had a tough decision. He sat on a bench in the park named for his great grandmother that overlooked Hendricks' riverfront holdings including the refrigerated warehouses used by local apple growers. Originally, they'd been ice houses. His family had owned the natural port that in the nineteenth century took delivery of all manner of

133

goods, including shiploads of Chinese porcelain, lead and copper ore, and whale oil, but now the port only received deliveries of fuel oil, diesel, and gasoline that was stored in large tanks right on the river's edge, leased to local oil companies by Lance's holding company.

But the Hendricks family, like most wealthy landed gentry in upstate New York, had never actually contributed much of anything to the town with the exception of when the Bradbury family, distant cousins who had been good friends of Ralph Waldo Emerson, donated some useless, swampy property along the river to found a school that eventually became Bradbury College.

To his credit, Lance had gone to a good law school, graduated near the middle of his class, and passed the bar on the first try. Running for DA had been his mother's idea. She was the daughter of Irish immigrants, and her generational family ambition was fresh off the boat, so she had revitalized the Hendricks line with a badly needed dose of intelligence and motivation.

As a major player in the local Republican and Conservative parties, Lance's mom had been instrumental in improving much of the tired old town, and had gotten new businesses and shops to open, including many owned by Hispanic immigrants, although, personally, she was not in favor of letting too many more immigrants into the country now that she was here.

Lance was sitting in his office talking to Jimmy, his campaign manager. He was up for reelection, and a young and ambitious attorney was running against him in the primary. In this town, whoever won the Republican primary won the race. The election in November was simply a formality. A Republican had held the position of DA since the end of the Civil War. Every now and then an earnest young lawyer would run as a Democrat, and he or she would campaign hard, would be very qualified, have excellent ideas, and be very well liked. But it would just never occur to anyone to actually vote for a Democrat.

The young, ambitious attorney, being wholly without imagination, was running on a law-and-order platform, as if the small college town ever had any real problem with crime. Other than an occasional student flirting with alcohol poisoning on a Friday night, or a local kid doing seventy in a thirty mile an hour zone, there was little crime to speak of — until lately. The terrorist who planted a bomb at the professor's house and insisted on dying needlessly on the highway caused some major excitement, and now that very same professor was accused of sexual harassment, which provided even more juicy stories for the usually very thin local paper. His opponent was making it look like a crime wave, which put Lance Hendricks in a place he absolutely hated: *he had to do something.*

Under normal circumstances, he would have been happy to let it slide. There was absolutely no evidence that the professor had done anything wrong; even a first-year law student would have known better than to make a charge. Lance also deferred to the college, since they had, over the years, become the major employer of the city simply because every other large business in town had either closed or offshored their operations.

That attitude, in fact, could have been a problem with a couple of previous cases where the college had certainly been guilty of covering up, among other things, sexual assaults. His lack of action had given them the impression that they could get away with pretty much anything they wanted, and that no matter what they did wrong, Lance's office would let it go. The young attorney with the help of that total pain in the ass Sasha Korbet was digging up every issue that his office had not aggressively pursued. It was more than a little hypocritical of Sasha Korbet because she knew the basic fact that no DA's office could prosecute every case that came along.

Korbet had her own "blind eye." She never made a big deal out of issues when his decisions supported her favored interests, such as when Lance's office decided not to pursue zoning issue violations for the nonprofit community theatre that had once been a factory and was in a zone that was strictly for business. The police also went easy on the parking tickets so people would shop. She didn't mention that his office had decided to not follow up on private property disputes related to the new rail/bicycle trail and chose to let the rail trail inherit an easement that had been explicitly only for the railroad.

All of this was flitting through Lance's mind when he addressed his campaign manager.

"What the hell, Jimmy?"

"Well said, Lance."

"There is no case. One anonymous Title IX complaint? That's all they've got? We could never take this to court."

"That's not the point. We're not talking about court or a trial. We're just talking about charging him. No judge will take this as a preliminary hearing since no one wants to look as if they are giving Bradbury another free pass, so send it to the grand jury and they can let him off. There's one empaneled right now; we can just throw this on their caseload. Blame them for letting the guy off, for being a bunch of liberal snowflakes on the grand jury. It can actually make you come off as stronger on law and order." Jimmy said, his voice serious, "You have to arrest him or you'll look like a wimp, and that Korbet bitch'll have your balls on a platter."

"I know. But it's so stupid. An assistant district attorney right out of law school would never bring charges on this evidence. Even the alleged victim isn't cooperating. She refuses to come forward, and I can't really compel her since she was underage, and technically we aren't even supposed to know who she is."

"That might be to our advantage, though," Jimmy mused. "She could be feeling very intimidated?"

"How so?"

"He might have threatened her?"

"With what? A bad grade? He's not even teaching the class anymore as I understand it."

"Well, just spreading a rumor might be enough. Just leak a rumor that there's evidence of intimidation. You don't have to back it up. People aren't that rational when it comes to validating their prejudices."

"The District Attorney's Office is not here to spread rumors."

"It is if you want to arrest this guy. And if you *don't* arrest him, it's going to look very bad for you. It's going to look like you're avoiding another sex case. But it'll be even worse. It could cost you the primary. You have to arrest him, even if you never bring him to trial."

***

Gil was in the attorney's office, the one he'd hired for Richard in what now seemed like a lifetime ago. Mike Miller had several photos hanging on his wall and a couple of excellent prints of famous Hudson River School paintings. Gil remembered them from the last time he'd been there with Claudia and Richard.

Miller was hunched over his desk looking at the papers in Gil's folder. He finished reading and looked up.

"I don't get it. This is all the evidence they have?"

"Apparently."

"Do you have any idea who the anonymous letter writer is?"

"I have my suspicions."

"Why would anyone go to this ... extreme?"

"Never worked on a college campus, have you?"

"No."

"The old saying is that the battles are so malicious because the stakes are so low," Gil said.

Mike chuckled. "Well, these stakes aren't low. If you get convicted, you wouldn't be able to continue teaching, not to mention possible jail time. I just don't see how Lance would do this. Unless it's political. He *is* running for office again this fall."

"Possibly," Gil said, and then thought about Millie and then thought about Gary. "Most definitely. But I have no idea why they want to bother with me. I just do my job. The idea that I would seduce one of my students, let alone one younger than my own daughter, is ludicrous. But if it's Gary and Millie behind this, and I think it is, then they'd never need much of a reason. Gary wants to be the next president of the college so badly that I wouldn't be surprised if he parades around at home in front of a mirror in his regalia calling himself Mr. President, and Millie's fine unless you disagree with her. Then she's your enemy for life."

"Bradbury also got a black eye from the last couple of high-profile sexual harassment cases. The fact that both got leaked to the press through social media, causing them to do a lot of backpedaling, might have made them a bit too anxious here. Maybe that's it, too?" the attorney volunteered. "In any case, they have to make this one anonymous report into a case, and I don't see that happening, especially if the girl won't make a complaint."

"Edith Frank?"

"She wouldn't by any chance be Libby Frank's daughter?"

"Yes." Gil said.

The lawyer was silent for a long moment before saying, "That might put a wrinkle in this case. It also might explain a thing or two."

"How so?"

"Libby might be insisting that this plays out all the way," he said. "But, while she can be aggressive, I've managed to beat her before. She's not the most careful of attorneys, not good with research, has a tendency to not do her homework, and counts too much on bluster and blow in the courtroom. Sometimes that works. Unfortunately, she wouldn't be dealing with this case anyway. It would be the DA's Office. And Lance Hendricks himself might prosecute this if it goes to trial." His eyes lost focus for a second as he thought. "But let's see what happens. They're bringing this to a grand jury first. It's not in your best interest to waive that right, so let's just go one step at a time."

# Chapter 27

Dr. Bill was outraged. He didn't like it when "his" college was portrayed in a bad light in the press, and the national news was having a great time filling in the gaps in their evening news with ten-second sound bites about Bradbury College and the ongoing scandal. Their satellite trucks were parked across the street from the main entrance to the campus, and more than one had asked his office for an interview, or at least a statement.

He was also upset with Lance Hendricks, a man he had campaigned for more than once, held fundraisers for on college property, and had helped out by throwing the power of the college behind him during his first primary.

The more conservative news outlets emphasized the book and the article that Gil had co-written with Valerie Dymond accusing Jefferson of stealing his ideas from a black pirate. They also made sure to include a picture of Val, just in case any of their viewers didn't already know that she was black. And then they repeatedly pointed out that one famous scholar who had challenged the facts behind the book, even though the conservative journalists didn't quite get the criticism straight. Lenny Trout had only pointed out that any direct link had to be assumed, that there was no provable direct connection between Jean's Charter for the *Rogue Noir* and Thomas Jefferson, which was something that Valerie and Gil had admitted in the book, so it wasn't even that much of a criticism. He never accused Gil and Valerie of "making the whole thing up," which was the conservative talking point. But such finesse of thought was beyond the press. Then they would shift very quickly to the charges of sexual harassment. That was where the more liberal press and the conservative press met with vengeance. No one seemed to notice the slenderness of the evidence, and they all took the opportunity to beat up on higher education.

Bradbury hadn't helped itself by getting caught trying to hide the fact that serious felonious sexual assaults had occurred on campus and had indeed been covered up. Stonewalling Sasha Korbet on the more recent cases had been their biggest mistake. She was a dedicated journalist with a pretty good bullshit detector. She picked Gary Sime for the ambitious climber that he was, since she was the same way, and had no intention of spending her career on a small city newspaper; she immediately knew that Gary would give anything to become the president of the college.

The quickest route to their goals was for her to break a national story and for Gary to discredit Dr. Bill so the trustees would have to ask for him to retire.

The ultra-conservative conglomerate MaxiNews had bought the local paper where Korbet worked, and, while they didn't dictate editorial policy, they were much inclined to quickly syndicate any story that promoted conservativism and so-called conservative family values. Any article painting higher education in a bad way was strongly encouraged, and any article that was critical of a professor was journalistic ambrosia. In short, Gil Sykes was the perfect steppingstone for both of them.

Dr. Bill looked out of his window, unseeing. He'd been given plenty of advice over the past few days, especially from Gary. He'd been suspicious of Gary for quite some time, and the photo on his phone that Christina had sent him confirmed it. Korbet had known things about the college before he did, and the details about the two previous cases were very accurate. Only someone at the higher executive level would have known the details that appeared in the newspaper.

Dr. Bill wasn't nearly as stupid as Gary thought he was. He picked up his phone and dialed the firm that was on retainer for the school and spoke at length with the senior partner who handled the college's legal matters. After about an hour he hung up the phone. A smile formed at the edges of his mouth but remained embryonic.

\*\*\*

Gary was in his office without a lot to do except get ready for a meeting that afternoon. He had wanted the school to throw Gil to the wolves as a sort of mea culpa for the previous cover ups; Dr. Bill thought it would be best to stand behind Sykes, especially since the evidence was so slim. Gary had the president in a difficult situation: either Dr. Bill stood behind a member of the faculty and an old friend, a fellow member of the white male elite, and ended up accused of contributing to another cover up—Gary would make certain that'd be how Sasha would hear it from him—or he fired Gil, which would certainly destroy his relationship with most members of the faculty, and possibly lead to a lawsuit. Either path could end up leading to Bill's retirement. Gary was pulling hard for the latter scenario; since he personally didn't care at all for Gil, he had no problem using a position of power to screw over people he didn't like.

Christina buzzed him on the intercom and told him that the president wanted to meet with him upstairs in his office in half an hour. Gary wondered what might be on his mind but smiled back at her and told her to confirm the meeting.

***

Dr. Bill's office was large and had an attached conference room. Since he was only meeting with Gary, his secretary led him into the inner office, which was paneled in oak and held a massive mahogany Chippendale desk, an intricately carved, opulent, and imposing chunk of furniture that had been donated by a trustee sometime in the 1950s. The president was on the phone finishing up a call, and motioned Gary to sit down.

"I just wanted to consult with you about the issue with Gil Sykes," Dr. Bill said as he hung up the phone. He didn't wait for Gary to respond. "There could be some damage here if we're not careful."

"Really?" Gary was intrigued.

"Yes." Dr. Bill focused his gaze outside the window, watching a barge go up the river preparing to dock at the port and offload gasoline at Hendricks' Wharf. "Unfortunately, there could be some records on Sykes buried in the archives that we probably don't want to become public."

"Really?" Gary had trouble sitting still.

"There were some ... misunderstandings that Sykes had with a few students, but that was a long time ago, and it's water under the bridge, so to speak. Now, I wasn't here at the time; it was before I was hired, so these are all allegations that we have to treat as completely unsubstantiated. Do I make myself clear?

"Gary nodded vigorously. "Of course, Bill."

"It's just that if any of it were to resurface now, then there could be some issues, and it wouldn't look good for Sykes, not at all, or the college. What was simply a case of mixed signals between a young professor and a couple of students years ago could be made into something really big now." Dr. Bill hesitated. "This should be kept quiet. You understand?"

"Of course," Gary responded, wondering if Sasha Korbet might be at her desk, but also wondering how to defer the blame if it were leaked.

As if to answer him, the president continued, "Only some of the older professors and administrative staff probably remember any of this, not to mention a few people who still work in Human Resources, and of course, the students, but they graduated years ago. That's why I can't believe Gil Sykes did this; I thought he'd learned his lesson." He looked straight at Gary and said, "Just want to bring you up to speed so you're not surprised by it if it comes out."

"I appreciate it, Bill."

"I just want to do the right thing, Gary."

"You can trust me, Dr. Bill."

"I'm sure of that," the president said, as his desk phone rang and he answered it in one smooth motion. He waved Gary out of his office while saying "hello" into the mouthpiece.

# Chapter 28

Mary was in her apartment on the phone talking to Paul. They'd been texting regularly, but she needed to talk directly to him, so she'd waited until she knew he'd be available. While she'd been teaching in Amsterdam, he'd been taking classes and working as an assistant in a lab at the University of Virginia. On a whim, Mary had asked him to go through the archives and see if any of Jefferson's papers were there, just to see what he could find.

She knew that Jefferson had been one of the founders of the University of Virginia, a school that had a library at the center instead of a chapel; the first secular university. Paul had told her that there was an extensive archive, but that Jefferson had sold his library to the government and some rare books to private dealers because he was chronically short of money. His papers were scattered in several places. Paul promised her he'd look in the archives. He called Mary as soon as he finished.

"I did manage to get into the library archives;" Paul said. "Lisa got me in and got me a special pass so no one would bother me."

Mary knew Lisa was a friend Paul had met near the start of the year. Mary felt a slight pang of jealousy when he mentioned her name. It was foolish, she chided herself. They had parted like adults, or so she thought. The feeling took her by surprise.

"Most of the papers here are from the time of the construction of the university, about 1818 or so," he said. "There could be some older stuff further back, but it's pretty much catalogued, and most of the older papers are from his two terms as president, which is long after the Declaration of Independence, and very long after he would have had contact with Jewel. Sorry. I'll be going back later this week and look through some more of his own personal papers. Some of them are a little older, but nothing before his five-year stay in France."

"I need to find something earlier than even that," Mary said thoughtfully.

"I know. Sorry."

"Don't apologize. It was a long shot at best."

"I'll go back later this week, maybe over the weekend," Paul said. He didn't want to get her hopes up, so he didn't tell her he'd found a promising-looking archival box that had the words Personal diary 1780s? penciled on the side. Unfortunately, he'd had to leave, but he set it aside on a library cart with a note to the librarians to not reshelf the box, and was hoping it would prove more fruitful than the hours he'd spent sifting through legal letters, correspondence, and drawings of the college — which was only a vision and an empty field at the time — and memos to his staff directing them on mundane daily affairs. Jefferson was a real micromanager.

They talked for a while, Paul about his research project and Mary talked about her students. Neither wanted to say goodbye, but Mary had to get ready to go out to dinner with her supervisor and some of the other teachers, and Paul was getting ready to go to class and then back to the lab. He promised to get in touch with her if he found anything at all of interest, and then they ended the call. But only because they had to.

***

Gil and Marion were home, where they'd spent most of their time since their problems started. Gil still went for his walks, and he had gotten very creative about ducking reporters, although they had thinned out. Now, however, their latest problem was staring at both of them in the evening newspaper and had been picked up by the major news services. An unnamed source had said that Gil had been accused of molesting at least two students in the past, but the good-old-boy network had covered it up. The DA's office was launching a thorough investigation.

"I don't know what to say, Marion. I have no idea where they could have gotten this. It's completely false."

"I don't, either," Marion's voice was brittle.

"You don't believe this, do you?"

"I don't know what to believe anymore," Marion said. "I was busy running back and forth to New York City while you were getting tenure. I have no idea what you were doing."

"Changing diapers, teaching, and writing like a madman, in that order. That's what I was doing."

"There's just so much going on. There's that guy on the TV show who has an affidavit that says you and Valerie were together all night at the hotel, and then I remembered that your phone was off all night. Hell, you didn't even get back to me until the next day. Where were you?"

"I told you. I shut my phone off because I was going to presentations all day, including Val's, and I don't want to bother anyone with my phone. Then we went to see a movie. It started at ten and wasn't over until midnight. I couldn't sleep, so we had a drink, and then I slept in late, forgot that my phone was off, and almost missed my plane. After that, it was off during the flight home. Since I never turn it on when I'm flying anyway, I just left it off." He stopped to take a deep breath. "It never occurred to me that there was another Richard crisis going on, as it turned out, his last. And this stuff about Edith Frank is nutty.

"These allegations are completely false. I have no idea where they came from. You saw how they took that picture of you and your niece in front of Planned Parenthood and made a huge fuss about it when it was really nothing? That's what these disgusting people do for a living: spin the truth, or simply outright lie."

"I know." She sounded very tired. "It's not you. I believe you. It's just that I … have to go."

"What?"

"I'm going to visit my sister. I need to get away."

"Claudia?"

"No, my other sister, Janice."

"You're going to Denver? Has she forgiven you for getting her daughter's picture on national TV?"

"I don't know, don't care. I'm sick of not going out, and of the stares in the grocery store. I've had enough." She sighed. "I bought a ticket last week. I leave tomorrow. Sorry, I can't take this anymore. I just have to get away. Go someplace where no one knows me."

"Wow."

They sat in silence for a while, and then Marion went into the bedroom. He heard her pull out her suitcase and rummage through her dresser and closet as she packed. He walked into the room. "How long will you be gone?"

"Not sure. Maybe a couple of weeks," she said. "I haven't really seen Janice in a while. Even when she comes here, we seemed to spend most of our time dealing with Claudia."

"That's true."

There was a long silence.

"I just need to get away."

"Yeah, you said that already."

"Sorry."

"Want me to drive you to the airport?"

"I can hire a car."

"No problem. It's not like I'm doing anything."

"Okay. Sorry."

"Me. too," he said. "Look on the bright side. With you gone, I'm free to molest young women to my heart's content."

"Stop, Gil. That's not funny."

"Nothing seems to be funny right now. Even if this gets cleared up and I go back to work, the bored minions who are willing to believe anything—or, rather, unable to disbelieve whatever nonsense they get fed—will never be convinced that I didn't do anything."

"You have more friends than you think you do, and those who know you know better," Marion said.

"Really? Well, where the hell are they?"

Marion knew better than to answer.

# Chapter 29

Mary took a cab from Charles de Gaulle airport to the *Archives Nationales*. The drive took about an hour. She went up to the main desk where a woman was working over a computer screen.

"*Bonjour, Madame,*" Mary said. "*J'appele au sujet de l'archivage d'informations sur Thomas Jefferson.*"

"*Oui,*" she replied. "You must be the American who called last week."

"Yes," Mary said.

"Do you prefer English or French?"

"English is fine if it's not too much trouble?"

"Your French is very good, but English is fine for me."

"Thank you."

She led Mary to a small room, and then told her to wait. Library aides had been assigned to get the materials she'd asked for. Since none of it had been scanned and put online, Mary would have to go through each box. Paul had found a few very short references in one of Jefferson's diaries from when he'd left France after being in Paris for five years.

Mary remembered the conversation. It had been her idea for Paul to look through the archives at the University of Virginia; she hoped there might be some papers in the archives that referenced the Charter, or, with luck, the Charter itself. Paul's search proved to be a dead end, except for a short reference from a journal Jefferson kept when he was in Paris.

"He was in Paris for five years as ambassador," Paul said. They were talking on the phone; she had gotten a discount sim card that gave her unlimited international minutes.

"So you think he had the Charter in Paris?"

"Could be, and that might be a big problem for you. He thought he was going back in about a year, as soon as he cleared up some issues in Monticello. But then Washington created the post of Secretary of State and gave it to Jefferson, so that put an end to his travels to France and other places in Europe. He never got to go back to Paris."

"Well, there was the French Revolution, too. That made travel to France, even for an American revolutionary, very dangerous."

"True, when he left to go back to the U.S., Napoleon was still just another corporal."

"Amazing how quickly the whole thing happened, the Revolution and then the Reign of Terror, then Napoleon. It must have been a frightening time."

"At this point, it's anyone's guess what could have happened to any personal papers he left in Paris. I hope you find something in the archives. It could be that many of the people he knew in Paris were either killed or left the country."

"I had hoped we'd have more clues by now."

"Sorry I couldn't be of more help here in Virginia."

"You helped me a lot. I owe you for sure."

"Good luck."

"Thanks," she hung up feeling a little less anxious, but suddenly she really knew that finding the Charter of the *Rogue Noir* in any of the archives that held Jefferson's papers would be challenging at best—or maybe impossible.

What Mary could piece together was that Jefferson came back home with several more people than he'd originally left with, including Sally Hemings. There hadn't been enough room to bring all that he had accumulated, so he'd left several cases of his own personal papers with the intention of collecting them the following year when he returned to his duties as ambassador.

Mary knew that she was taking a real long shot. The papers had been left in the care of a friend who had been one of the tutors for his daughter and Sally Hemings. When Mary checked on his name, Marc Legrande, she found that he'd left for England not long after the French Revolution. He was a distant relative of a nobleman, and even though his sympathies were probably much more with the revolutionaries than the monarchy, such fine distinctions were not drawn when it came to fodder for the guillotine. She speculated that Legrande likely didn't take the time to carry along Jefferson's papers, since he was fleeing for his life. He died a few years after going to England of typhoid. She knew the chances of her finding what she was looking for were pretty slim.

The library aides came to her wheeling a cart with several acid-free boxes. Mary began with the nearest.

***

Gil woke up early, not having slept very well in the first place. Marion had called the night before, and they'd talked for a while. She didn't mention coming back, although it had been more than two weeks since she'd flown to Denver. The presentation to the grand jury had been postponed pending the results of the DA's investigation into the new allegations. Today was the day that he'd have to be at the court, but Mike Miller, his attorney, had advised him not to appear before the grand jury. Mike had explained to him, that it was the burden of the prosecution to convince the majority of the jury that there was enough evidence to bring charges. He also said that his inside information and his own careful review of the evidence showed that they had very little, but cautioned that, as Gil knew, the case was extremely political. He'd seen more than one indictment returned on scant evidence because of the underlying politics.

Gil met Mike at the courthouse. They were put in a waiting room. Gil had brought a book to read but couldn't concentrate. Mike had some papers he was working on.

He looked at Gil. "I still think it best to not volunteer to go in front of this jury. They can ask you anything at all, and you could get nervous and say something that gets misinterpreted," Mike said. "It wouldn't be the first time."

"I understand," Gil said. "But you know the saying about a DA able to get a grand jury to indict a ham sandwich?"

"Sure. This is entirely the prosecution's ballgame, but they can't let hearsay evidence in, which means the letter is out, and that's the main pillar of their case." Mike sat back. He continued thoughtfully, "I've seen it when innocent people cause big problems for themselves. They act nervous or fidgety in front of twenty-three people all asking them questions. They look guilty even though they aren't, and then they volunteer information that seems incriminating. In fact, it's more likely that an innocent person who had never been in trouble would actually act nervous and fidgety—guilty. I've seen an experienced criminal who'd been in trouble many times before be as cool as can be in front of a judge or a jury, and act like he had no idea why anyone would even think that he would break the law." He winked. "Not that any of my clients have ever been guilty."

"Of course not." Gil smiled.

\*\*\*

Lance surveyed the grand jury. Most of them were older, retired people. Younger people simply could not give up the time to work essentially for free for six weeks, unless they had a job that would pay them while serving, and few people had those sorts of jobs. He decided to bring the Sykes case up first. He called the first witness, an investigator from the DA's Office, an officer of the court, who was appointed to the case to look at related charges raised in an article in the local newspaper, although Lance would have done this as a matter of routine anyway with or without a newspaper making the allegations. The officer was sworn in.

"So, Officer, can you explain what you did and what you found?"

"I investigated Mr. Sykes by looking through his Human Resources file at Bradbury College going back to the year he started, and by interviewing previous students of his, colleagues and staff. My investigation took me back over fifteen years, and I managed to locate and interview about thirty of his former students."

"What did you find regarding any sexual harassment charges?"

"Nothing at all."

"Nothing?"

"He has had two campus parking violations," the officer said. Members of the grand jury laughed. "I found nothing in his record at all, and most of the students I interviewed said he was a good teacher, and that was it. As far as I could determine, he never touched one of his students, nor did he even have a reputation for socializing with them. I interviewed both men and women, some of whom took a class with him over ten years ago. Most said only good things about him, although there were a few complaints."

"About what?" Lance asked.

"Many of them didn't like their final grades."

The grand jury laughed again. Lance didn't mind, since he was hoping that they would not vote to indict, which would let him off the hook. The last thing he wanted was to bring this to trial. This way he could simply shrug and point to the grand jury during the inevitable outrage from the uninformed and ignorant "experts" on TV talk shows that would follow.

"So there is no evidence at all?"

"None that I could find."

"Even unofficially?"

"No. In these cases, if there is a problem and it becomes public, then a lot of others who were harassed usually come forward. Like when a noted TV personality or movie star is accused, there's a stream of people who suffered abuse who come forward."

"Like the Me, Too movement?"

"Yes, and the ultimate test is if the abused come forward and their stories are similar. Abusers tend to use the same patterns. Nothing of the sort happened here."

What if the records are inaccurate?" Lance asked.

"Good question. Records can be manipulated. I look for unexplained gaps in the physical records, missing yearly evaluations, references to hearings that have no minutes, things like that."

"And."

"Nothing," the officer said.

"Anything else?"

"I always go for what I call the buzz factor. Basically, is there a common perception that someone, a teacher, doctor, colleague, et cetera, is someone you should stay away from. Knowledge of a sexual harasser is handed down from older students or staff members to the newer staff."

"You mean they warn them off? Stay away from so and so?"

"Exactly. Or they might have a nickname like the perv, or handyman, something like that."

"And?"

"Again, nothing. No pattern of abuse, no cover-up, no collective buzz, nothing."

"Thank you."

Lance let the grand jury ask questions, and then called his next witness.

Gary Sime took the stand and smiled at the grand jury. Lance reviewed his notes. Gary had been interviewed by one of his assistant district attorneys and he had noted that Sime had volunteered as a character witness.

"How long have you known, and how would you describe the accused?"

"Gil?" Gary said, "I've known him for about five years, ever since I started at Bradbury. He's always been a good teacher who handled his students well."

"Could you elaborate?"

"Well, he's taught the same course for a long time, and the students like to take it for a general education credit. And he's done a great job with it," Gary added purposely with a slight drop in his voice.

"Have you ever had any problems with him?"

"No. Not me."

"Some have?"

"I'd rather not say."

"This is a grand jury. You have to say," Lance said, beginning to be a little concerned. He noted the name on the fact sheet in front of him and groaned quietly. The interviewer was the son of one of the council members, a nice guy who just barely made it through law school, not the sharpest knife in the drawer. He was charged with writing the new regulations for signage in the town, but had done it so poorly that almost every business in town would have had to remove their signs, along with the state and federal government signs on the highway and for the local parks; all of them would have been in violation of his regulations. The council quietly paid another attorney to fix the regulations before they voted. That's when he became Lance's problem. Lance only let him handle contested speeding tickets and other minor traffic court issues. He began to wonder what Gary's agenda was, but now it was too late.

"Gil is a fine teacher and a good researcher. He really has been an asset to the college for a very long time ... as long as you let him do things his own way. He's certainly not a team player."

"But that's not a crime? What is the relevance here?"

"Oh, nothing at all, but he has a tendency to keep very much to himself. Never goes to mixers or any of those sorts of events. I always wondered what he had to hide. Let's say that we didn't always see eye to eye."

"That, again, is not a crime, is it, Mr. Sime? Is there some sort of rule that he had to show up at these events?" Lance asked.

Then one of the jurors asked a question. "Is there anything that makes you think that Professor Sykes did actually do anything wrong?"

"No," Gary said. "Not me. I didn't want to take any action on that letter, but my hands were tied."

There was complete quiet in the room. Lance could hear all of them at once silently ask "what letter?" It was hearsay, and the laws of New York State actually forbade it being introduced, although more than one prosecutor had managed to work around the law and get information to the grand jury that they were not supposed to. Now that it had been mentioned, Lance knew that the grand jury would subpoena the document. The best he could do was to present it himself.

"The letter he refers to is an unsigned accusation that was written by a third party about the alleged victim that does not mention Professor Sykes by name. There is no signature, and there is no actual mention of either the victim or the perpetrator by name. As I have repeatedly said, the alleged victim has not made any accusations. The letter is hearsay and not something that would normally be admitted to the grand jury."

"I agree one hundred percent. That letter is of no consequence." Gary said.

*But you certainly went out of your way to make it so.*

After Gary was excused, Lance found the letter in his file and presented a copy of it to the grand jury.

He was careful to explain the rules of evidence and that this document was complete hearsay and could never normally be admitted in a court of law, and as such it needed to be treated with a strong dose of skepticism.

He then called two more witnesses who testified that they had never seen Gil and the student together in any context other than on campus or in a classroom, although one did mention that she had seen the alleged Jane Doe run out of Gil's office in tears. While not hearsay, Gil had actually mentioned this in his own statements, and had said he had no idea why Edith was behaving that way, although there was a record of him informing campus counseling services.

The grand jury couldn't resist a good juicy scandal, or injecting a conspiracy where none existed, and seemed incapable of being skeptical of anything that required the use of common sense—or facts. They returned an indictment against Gilbert Sykes for the crime of felony sexual harassment.

Lance made a mental note to assign the ADA who had screened Gary Sime to the job of scanning all of the county files going back to the nineteenth century in order for them to be compliant with the current New York State initiative on digital archives of all public records, a pet project of a newly appointed deputy assistant attorney general. Lance hoped that it would take the blithering idiot the rest of his career.

# Chapter 30

Valerie Dymond looked at her phone thoughtfully for a minute before placing the call. She was in the middle of her living room, packing boxes with books. She'd already packed her clothes, and she had far more books than clothes. Gil answered on the second ring.

"Hi, Val."

"Hi, Gil. I just wanted to touch base with you and see how you're doing."

"I'm okay, considering, and you?"

"Packing up. I'm moving in with my fiancé. Didn't want you to just call and find out that I was gone."

"He's in North Carolina, right?"

"Yeah."

"I can't believe they just fired you like that. How do they justify it?"

"They don't, not really. There was some nonsense about inadequate publications, and misuse of grant money, this from the same college where professors retire who haven't published an article since they got tenure, not to mention the dean who took a grant from a private foundation earmarked for a jazz program and used it to pay the salary of a visiting classical concert pianist because he personally doesn't like jazz."

"Why am I not surprised? It's pretty typical. It's like Claude Raines in *Casablanca*, 'I'm shocked to see gambling in this establishment!'"

"Your winnings, sir." Valerie laughed, finishing the line.

"Right. Is there anything you can do?"

"Don't worry about me. I have an attorney and she's filing a lawsuit. There's plenty of evidence that they pulled a rabbit out of their hat for this one, and while I don't like to play the race card, I think it might have had something to do with it. Would they have done this to a white male? Or any male for that matter?" She took a quick breath and continued, "Meanwhile, though, I need a place to stay. Unemployment insurance doesn't go very far, especially here, so it looks like I move to Durham. I was already looking for jobs there anyway. My fiancé makes twice my salary. It would never make any sense for him to move up here. How about you?"

"The trial is next week, and my attorney says they have no case. But, to be honest, he'd also said that I wouldn't be indicted, so it's anyone's guess."

"Sorry,"

"Not your fault."

"I feel that it is."

"Don't," Gil said.

"Take care, Gil," Val said after a long silence. "I'll call you after I get settled. Maybe you and Marion can come down for a visit?"

"You, too, Val. And if you find a job, tell them you have a friend who's looking, too." He heard her laugh as he hung up. His phone buzzed again. He hadn't had a phone call in three days, except for the occasional telemarketer or other unknown number, and now he'd had two, one right after the other.

The call was from Marion. She asked him to pick her up at the airport. She'd be flying in from Colorado and would arrive around nine that night.

***

Mary was digging through the last box of records. She had cotton gloves on so the oil from her hands wouldn't come into contact with the valuable papers. This was her third day in the archives with still no luck. The last box seemed to be mostly receipts from a trip Jefferson took to Provence and to Italy. Some works she'd read said it was to get over a romantic involvement with the beautiful artist Maria Cosway after she went back to England with her husband. In any case, there was no Charter, not one document that even resembled the language of the Declaration of Independence.

Mary checked the time. She'd brought her suitcase to the archives and had checked it in a locker wanting to devote as much time as possible to looking for the Charter before she absolutely had to leave. Now she needed to get to the airport and head back to Amsterdam for work the next morning. Calling a cab, she reluctantly placed the top back on the last acid-free box and walked to the front desk to retrieve her suitcase.

On the plane she got a call from Paul, but she let it go to voicemail and sent him a text telling him she'd call him when she landed. Roaming charges using the plane's Wi-fi were too much for her budget. On the bus to her apartment, she called him.

"Any luck?" he asked.

"No, not really. Mostly boring personal papers that had obviously already been perused by every person who has ever written a book about Jefferson during his Paris days," she said. There was a long pause where she thought the phone might have disconnected. "Hello?"

"I'm still here. Sorry. I was trying to think of something positive to say."

"That's what I like about you: you're sweet."

"It doesn't help though, does it?"

"Maybe. Anyway, how are things going?"

"Not bad. I found a cool person to research for my thesis." He sounded excited.

"Who?"

"Not many people know of him. He was an assistant for Eric Erikson and was deeply involved with many of the clinical trials that Erikson's famous for. He actually set up some of the experimental protocols. He died young, though, I think from cancer, before he could get out on his own and make a name for himself, but what he left in his personal papers is excellent. The guy was brilliant, so there's certainly enough for a thesis, and maybe even a dissertation. I'm still not sure if I want to go all the way to a Ph.D."

"That sounds great," Mary said with a twinge of jealousy. Her year off had left her out of the paper chase, and she hadn't given a moment's thought to writing a thesis or conducting a clinical experiment at all. Paul was talking about the research he'd done so far, and Mary was half listening to him when she suddenly slapped herself on the forehand. Paul stopped talking.

"What was that?"

"The sound of my stupidity," Mary said, checking the time. It was too late to call the archives, but she would first thing in the morning.

"Care to enlighten me?"

"Yes and no. It might be a dead end. In fact, it's probably a dead end, so I won't get my hopes up. But I'll call you as soon as I know." She changed the subject. "Your thesis topic sounds great. Makes me want to get right back to work, too, but I still don't know which direction to go."

"You'll figure it out, but you know your strength is in talking to people. Unlike most psychology students you're actually very good with real, tangible people. You'd be miserable in a lab."

"Yeah." She knew he was right. "Thanks, Paul."

"My pleasure," he said. "I hope things work out for your dad. He seems like a nice guy."

"He is."

"My dad's an absolute asshole. Nothing bad happens to him or guys like him. The system seems designed to automatically protect them, or even promote them. The assholes of the world always seem to be doing fine."

"That's true." More silence. "Bye, Paul."

"Later, Mary."

Mary put a reminder in her smartphone calendar to call the archives and make another appointment but knew she wouldn't possibly forget.

# Chapter 31

A wagon and two small carriages were parked in front of the *Hôtel de Langeac*. The wagon was loaded to the point where it almost rested on the axles. The four large, powerful horses would need all they could muster to haul it to the docks on the Seine. Five people stood in the doorway, three men and two women.

"I will miss you, *mon ami*," Marc Legrande said.

"I will miss you, too, Marc," Jefferson replied, and patted the man on the shoulder of his expensive jacket. Marc was dressed as a professional, a teacher; his clothes, with his tight-fitting, colorful vest, and puffy white silk shirt, were far fancier than Jefferson's, who wore the plain, unpretentious clothes he always insisted on. While the court had gotten used to Jefferson's taste in clothing, Marc still found it a little unsettling.

Marc approached Sally Hemings.

*"N'oubliez pas de pratiquer votre Français tous les jours."*

*"Mais oui,"* she replied to her teacher, smiling. She and her brother James got into one of the carriages, and they waited to leave. Jefferson helped his daughter into the other carriage.

"No more convent schools for you, Patsy. It's time to dilute the all that papal influence." Thomas turned to Marc. "I'm afraid that I have to ask you for one more favor, even though you have been more than helpful to all of us."

"Whatever you wish, Thomas."

"As you can see, the wagon and carriages are all loaded with as much as we dare carry. I'm sure the captain will not be happy with all of this extra cargo. I've made arrangements for shipping the rest of my belongings home, but there are four large boxes of my papers still in the library of the house. Could you store them for me? I will be back in six months, certainly no longer than a year; I am confident that my affairs at Monticello should be resolved soon after I get back, and this insurgency here, if it happens at all, will be over very shortly. I think you will probably end up with a constitutional monarchy. There is no need for bloodshed. I'm positive that it will be peaceful."

"But of course," Marc said. He bid them all goodbye again, and the carriages started for the docks. He went into the empty house and found four wooden boxes neatly stacked in a corner. Marc sent his servant to hire a carriage to take them to his house. While waiting, he opened the nearest box. Among the neatly stacked papers tied in bundles with cotton twine, there was a round leather case. He opened it and pulled out a rolled vellum document tied with a piece of green silk.

# Chapter 32

Gil and Mike sat in the courtroom waiting for the proceedings to start. There was a larger audience than usual in the gallery, but they'd expected it. Mike had said that the trial would be short since there was so little evidence to present. The prosecution had few witnesses, and the young woman, the alleged victim, had refused to cooperate with either the prosecution or the defense. Mike had dozens of letters from friends vouching for Gil Sykes and was hoping the judge would admit them into evidence and pass them on to the jury.

They all rose as Judge Jayne Service entered the courtroom.

She addressed the jury, concluding with, "It is up to you to seek justice, and our measure for this is beyond a reasonable doubt. That does not mean beyond all doubt. The burden of proof lies with the prosecution. If the prosecution has convinced you beyond a reasonable doubt, then you must find the defendant guilty. If you feel that the prosecution has not made its case, then you must find the defendant not guilty.

"Mr. Hendricks, your opening statement?"

Lance Hendricks started with a short address to the jury about the fact that parents send their young people and trust colleges and universities across the country to teach them what they will need to have a successful life. Betrayal of that trust through sexual harassment was, he propounded, the worst sort of betrayal, the same as a priest or a doctor betraying a member of his flock or his patient, and anyone who commits such a betrayal should be punished to the fullest measure of the law.

Mike said in his opening that he was in full agreement with the prosecutor, and that anyone who sexually harassed a person under his or her care should be punished. However, that was what the trial was all about, and he aimed to show that his client did not do anything like what he was charged with, had no history of such behavior, and that the alleged victim herself has refused to come forward and name him as the culprit. He threw up his hands for good measure as if to say, "I have no idea what we're all doing here in the first place."

The prosecution started by calling their own investigator to the stand. Lance knew that if he didn't call him, the defense would; otherwise he would have not bothered. Nothing the investigator was going to say would help his case. The officer made essentially the same testimony that he made before the grand jury. There was no evidence of wrongdoing in any of the files going back during Gil's entire career at Bradbury, nothing other than two parking tickets.

Then Lance threw a potential curveball. "Is it possible that any evidence of wrongdoing could have been purged from the record?"

"Yes. That's always a possibility."

"So your report can't conclude that there was no cover up?"

"No report can conclude that."

"Thank you. No further questions, Your Honor," Lance said.

"Cross?" asked the judge.

"How long have you been an investigator for the District Attorney's Office?" Mike asked the witness.

"Ten years."

"Have you ever come across official records that had been tampered with? Where information had been changed to keep you from finding out the truth?"

"Yes. It does happen. I always have to dig deeper than the official records."

"How do you find that out? That there's been an attempt to throw you off the trail?"

"There are many methods. People think they're being really clever, when they're really being stupid. Sometimes it's pretty obvious that pages are missing from a report that's made every few months or even every year, or that some parts of a report have been rewritten, but the best way to do an investigation such as this is to interview people who were there and would have firsthand knowledge about the events. And if what they say does not gel with the official reports, then I dig deeper."

"Did you do that with this investigation?"

"Yes, I did. I interviewed dozens of former students and colleagues, administrators who worked with HR, and people who knew the defendant during the period he was alleged to have committed the crimes. It's not that I was suspicious of a coverup, it's just good practice."

"What did you find?"

"There was no evidence at all that Professor Sykes had any history at all of assaulting students. And there was no evidence at all of any coverup. All the records were in order. If there *had* been a cover up, it wouldn't extend to people who have long since left the school. And there is usually what I call folklore."

"Meaning?"

"Whatever is covered up is usually common knowledge. People aren't stupid. Older students or employees tell younger ones not to be alone with Mr. X, or to be careful if Mr. Y is coaching your team. There was none of that here."

"What initiated the investigation?"

"As far as I know, a newspaper story that quoted an unnamed source alleging that there had been a coverup of sexual harassment committed by Gilbert Sykes several years ago by Bradbury College."

"Was there any other story that was published or broadcast by any other news source making the same claims? Anything that corroborated the story?"

"No. Nothing that added new information. All of them simply took the article off the wire service and repeated it or boiled it down for broadcast. There was no other source of the allegations."

"In your expert opinion was there any evidence that professor Sykes molested any student ever in his career at Bradbury College?

"No."

"And is there any evidence that the college was involved in a coverup?

"No."

"Thank you, that will be all, Your Honor," Mike addressed the judge.

"Mr. Hendricks, redirect?" Judge Service asked.

"No, thank you, Your Honor."

Lance called two other witnesses, a professor who had an office on the same floor as Gil's who said that the alleged victim was seen running from Gil's office, and Gary Sime, who played the same game he played before in the grand jury and managed to mention the letter in spite of Mike Miller's objection, and also managed to work it in that he too had seen the girl running from Gil's office, but had chosen not to say anything up until then.

Only this time the judge would not allow the note in evidence even though Lance tried to invoke more than one exception to the hearsay rule.

She ruled the letter inadmissible and instructed the jury to ignore all reference to it.

Gary Sime didn't notice that Dr. Bill, who had been called as a character witness for Gil, was in the audience, nor did he notice the expression on the president's face.

Mike had gone over with Gil that their only strategy was to bring character witnesses forward testifying that Gil Sykes would never do the thing he was accused of, but that doing so always carried some risk. "No one's a complete Boy Scout," he'd said. He was also leery of Gil taking the stand on his own behalf, since he had seen previous clients become their own worst enemies once cross examined by a prosecutor.

Mike concluded that his best option was to ask the judge to dismiss the case on the grounds of insufficient evidence.

He estimated that if Justice Service ruled against them, and didn't dismiss the charges, they had an even chance of winning. Mike made the motion to dismiss as soon as Lance finished with his last witness.

Judge Service had been expecting it and took her time. If the case had been a normal one, she would have dismissed it outright for lack of evidence, but because of the media circus surrounding it, and the relentless trial by press that had already occurred, she knew that such a move would bring charges of corruption and favoritism to her court. Like every other court judge, she had to run for reelection. The jury had to find him either guilty or not guilty; anything else would look like a coverup. She ruled against dismissal and called for a recess until the next morning.

That evening and the next morning most of the print and online press summed up the first day of the trial with the phrase: "Yes, that's always a possibility, investigator says in court."

***

"Are you out of your mind? You will not go to that court and testify. You'll never get into Harvard Medical School if your name gets dragged into this mess. If you walk into that courtroom, you lose all plausible deniability. No first-tier medical school will touch you." Libby Frank was fuming.

"And who started the mess, Mom?" Edith said. "I told you when you came to me in the hospital to leave it alone, but you had to push, like you always do. You have to know everything. And you have to control everything even if you have no idea what the fuck is going on! Do you ever check the facts before you fucking jump in?"

"Don't use that language with me," Libby said.

"Don't play lawyer with me and try to change the subject. You brought this *mess* on by pushing buttons and pushing people around, as you usually do, and now it looks like Professor Sykes might go to jail. And he had nothing to do with it."

"He will be fine," Libby said. "The jury will let him off."

"Really? Have you been reading the papers, Mom? Have you tuned into even one of those talk shows, or the online press? They want his blood, if only to keep up their ratings."

"Don't believe everything you read in that rag, especially that crap Sasha Korbet writes."

"I don't. But if you believe half of what she's writing, then it doesn't look good. She's been all but saying that he's guilty as hell, and you know that people can get convicted on almost no evidence when it gets political like this case." She ran her fingers through her hair and added,

"People will convict him because they feel they have no choice, or they just don't like the college, or teachers in general." Her tone turned even angrier as she said, "I *would* like to know who wrote that letter accusing him of molesting me. Now that is the person who should go to jail."

Her mom fell curiously silent after Edith finished talking, a fact that wasn't lost on Edith. She'd had her suspicions.

"I'll talk to Lance Hendricks," Libby offered softly. "I started out as a prosecutor working for him. He'll listen to me. He's a fair man, and certainly wouldn't want to convict someone who's innocent." She patted her daughter's multicolored hair. Edith pulled away.

"Not this time, Mom. If you won't tell me who wrote that letter, and I know you know, then I'll have to figure it out myself. I'm not one of your clients, and I'm certainly not on a jury that you're trying to dupe, so cut the bullshit.

"I know Lance Hendricks, and he might not be the brightest district attorney in the state but has put plenty of people in jail. That's what he does for a living, Mom, in case you haven't noticed. That's his job. That's how he gets reelected. Whether someone is innocent or guilty is beside the point. He gets voted in because he puts people in jail, usually black or brown people so no one gives a shit. He does it so that he can look tough on crime, and you know that's true because you've said it often enough. Stop treating me like I'm a child."

Libby sat, staring at the marble counter, and then Edith picked up her car keys and strode to the door.

"Wait."

"Why? So you can try to bullshit me again?"

"No."

"It was a letter given to Gary. Vice President Sime."

"That man's a total simpering ass."

"I know it, but he can be a useful simpering ass," Libby said, then continued, "It was written by one of Gil Sykes's teaching assistants, some young guy named Paul? Pat? Something like that? Anyway, Gary was a little light on the details. I see now that he was trying to impress me; I was pushing for a result, and he obliged. I'm sorry that—" Libby looked at Edith's face, which had changed to a mask of pure disgust "What's?" she asked her daughter but had already met the truth halfway. Edith's expression was enough.

"My God! Do you have any idea how you were played? I thought you were supposed to be a good lawyer."

"Sorry."

"Tell that to Gil Sykes," Edith said. "I can't believe that you'd unhesitatingly think I'd have sex with a man Dad's age but it wouldn't even cross your mind that I'd fuck a good looking graduate assistant who just happened to teach one of my discussion groups? What sort of emotional basket case do you think I am?"

Without another word, she left the kitchen, the custom-made storm door closing behind her, the pneumatic closer too civilized to let it slam shut, as much as she wished otherwise.

# Chapter 33

Gil and Marion were at her favorite restaurant, Gino's. She hadn't been there since Claudia had taken her out for lunch in what seemed like years ago, even though it had only been a few months. She and Claudia had spoken on the phone a couple of times, but they hadn't gotten together. Richard was still lodged between them, and would be for a while, perhaps forever. Marion and Gil hadn't talked very much, but she'd been in the courtroom that day for the trial. Neither of them was very hungry, but neither wanted to make dinner. Going out had been Gil's idea, and she knew they had to be brave. It was clear that a few people had recognized Gil. Some were pointing and looking, but he'd had long since gone past the point of caring, or even noticing.

Gil was glad she was there, but he was still angry with her for going away in the first place, although part of him understood.

He noticed an angry-looking man approaching their table, and he stopped eating.

"I have a daughter," the man said.

"So do I," Gil replied.

"Then you should know better."

"Than what?" Gil said coolly.

"You pretending you don't know?"

"I'm not pretending anything. For one thing, I don't even know you, and you certainly don't know me."

"I don't hang out with child molesters," the man snarled.

"That makes two of us. Now, can I finish my dinner, or should I call for someone to throw you out? Or better yet, should I just call the police?" Gil said, reaching for his phone. The man looked as if he wanted further confrontation but backed off and left the restaurant. His wife had been waiting for him by the door. She looked down at her feet, looking embarrassed and resigned. Gil thought she probably spent a lot of time apologizing for her husband, enabling him, making excuses for her bruises.

"Wow. I thought he was going to hit you," Marion said.

"Me, too. I was getting ready to duck."

"I'd already dialed 911 and was just ready to hit the send button."

"Smart. I was beginning to wonder how I was going to dial 911 with him pounding on my head."

"Jesus, Gil." Gino, the former Bradbury teacher-cum-restaurant owner, had come from the back. "I'm so sorry!" I'm going to remember that asshole, and he's not going to be allowed in here again. I'm sorry. So sorry."

"It wasn't your fault, Gino," Gil said.

"Not just that." He waved his hand in the direction of the table that the man had been seated with his wife. "The whole thing. For goodness sake, who would believe this at all? You? Molesting students? What the hell is wrong with people today?"

"I hope that the people on the jury all agree with you."

"I can't see how it could go any other way."

"You don't read the paper?"

"I do, but that reporter's obviously got issues with you or the school. She's never written a good word about Bradbury yet."

"I hope other people see it that way, too," Gil said. "Thank you. You're one of the few people who have actually talked to us in the last couple of months."

"No one from Bradbury?"

"Nope. Just Christina. I go to her for massage therapy. You know her? She works in Sime's office?"

"Yes. She's a good person, treated me well when I was just a lowly part-timer. Not all of the staff is like that when it comes to dealing with the adjuncts."

"We should get together, Gino, let us cook for you for a change? But I'm not nearly as good as you are." Gil stifled a yawn. "I'm pretty exhausted, and have to be in court tomorrow morning, not that I think I'll sleep very much tonight. Can we settle up with you?" Gil reached for his wallet.

"Hell, no. This is on me."

"No. That's nice of you, but ...."

"Gil, it's the least I can do," Gino was firm, and Gil didn't argue further. He and Marion thanked him and then left.

As they walked through the parking lot, they noticed the paint. Rapist! and Child Molester! had been spray painted on someone's car in bright orange paint.

"Wow. Must have been our gutless friend," Gil said.

"It looks just like your old car," Marion said. "The one that got burnt up by the terrorist."

"Yes, it even has a Bradbury parking sticker. It's a different color, though. Mine was green, this one's blue."

"I wonder who owns it. Should we go in and find him?"

"Nah, let whoever it belongs to finish dinner in peace. He'll find out soon enough. I see that Gino has security cameras. Gil pointed to the camera on top of a pole pointing in the direction of the parking lot. "With the whole thing on video, even our local police will be able to figure it out. I need to get home."

Marion drove; Gil fell asleep in the car.

*** 

Peter Morton was working late. He had been a prep cook for Gino ever since he started graduate school. The stipend he got as a teaching assistant wasn't nearly enough to cover his expenses. It was close to midnight when he was finished with cleaning up his workstation and setting up for the next day's lunch shift; he had one glass of beer before he went out to the parking lot.

He had to look at his car several times under the mercury vapor lights, and he read and reread the messages in day-glow orange paint. Peter at first was enraged, but then fear began creeping in, pushing back the rage. Did someone know something? He'd heard about the jerk who'd bothered Gil earlier that evening, everyone on staff had talked about it the whole shift. He wondered whether this was a case of mistaken identity or if someone knew his secret.

He had decided to quietly drive away when Gino came out of the kitchen. Gino, too, had been familiar with Gil's old car. Even back in his teaching days, the vehicle had been a joke among the staff on campus. He made the connection as soon as he saw Peter's car and called the police. Gino went back into the restaurant and went to the hostess station to get the reservation book and gathered all of the charge receipts. He was going to find out who the asshole was and share that information with the police.

# Chapter 34

Edith drove around aimlessly, finally ending up at Jane's house. She texted her to see if she was home, and then went in. Jane met her at the door with a hello and a hug.

"It's nice to see you, Edee. I might be your classmate next year."

"Really?"

"Yes. Just got word that I'll be in the advanced bridge program. I'll still be a high school senior while you'll be a sophomore, but I'll be on campus most days." She pointed to a letter on the desk.

"Wow." Edith hugged her friend again. "That'll be great."

"Any reason you're here, or did you just drop by?"

"Both."

"What did your mom do this time?"

"Not really her. It's something I should have done." She told her about the guy she had gotten pregnant by. Jane already knew about the brief encounter and the subsequent abortion, but didn't really know who he was, other than his name was Peter. When Edith got to the part about the letter Peter wrote accusing Gil of seducing her, Jane's face contorted a little, and her jawline became more pronounced. Edith then went on to tell her about how her mother had said to stay out of it, that her name in the case would mess up her chances for medical school and would be in every news outlet in the country once she went public. Her name was confidential because of the nature of the case; testifying would let the genie out of the bottle.

"I knew your mom would be mixed up in it somewhere," Jane interrupted and said. "I've been reading about the case, and it seems like there's no real evidence, and, of course, I know for sure he didn't do it, although I didn't know exactly who Peter was. I've been wondering what the hell's going on."

"It's all political. Peter could be in a lot of trouble, especially since I was underage, so he pushed it off on Professor Sykes. Even the DA doesn't think he's guilty—at least that's what Mom says."

"So he's getting blamed because the school has a history of not doing the right thing in the first place?"

"Yeah, pretty much, and the article he worked on didn't help. I read it. It made a lot of sense to me. Who cares if Jefferson borrowed a phrase or two from someone else? It doesn't really change anything, does it?"

"Even you're not that naïve, Edee," Jane said. "Or are you?"

"I'm not naïve, Jane. But racism does tend to sneak up on me." She thought for a few seconds. "Maybe you're right. I do tend to think the best of people and that's why I'm always surprised, sometimes shocked."

"You can think the best of people if you want to, but just not all the time; you need to remember that they're human, too," Jane said. "So what are you going to do? That's what's important here."

"The right thing," Edith said and took out her cellphone, dialing the number she'd put in the contacts list on the day the trial started.

***

Mike Miller was scanning the courtroom, searching for someone. Gil was sitting next to him, afraid he might vomit. Mike saw who he was looking for and smiled. The judge entered the courtroom, and the trial resumed.

Mike approached the bench. "Your Honor, I have a surprise witness who has come forward. I would like to put her on the stand before I call my other witnesses, since this might save us all a lot of time."

The judge's eyebrows went up. "Lance," she said to the DA, who was already curious about what was going on, "come here, and we'll go to my chambers."

"Okay, Mike, let me know about this witness."

"It's Edith Frank, the woman who is the unnamed Jane Doe, the alleged victim."

"Is it okay with her mother?" she said with an ironic smile. "I'll need to talk with Edith first. I assume she's in the courtroom?"

"Yes."

"Have the bailiff bring her here. Lance, do you have any objections?"

"Not yet, but I want to know the grounds."

"She's already been named in the transcripts and in the original charges, but only as Jane Doe, an anonymous student. Since she *is* Jane Doe, she can be called as a surprise witness. It's within the rules," Mike said.

"Does she realize this'll mean she's no longer anonymous? Trials are all public information. Her name will be in the news. Even if I put a gag order on it, that's not really going matter," Judge Service said.

"Yes. I told her yesterday when she called me," Mike replied.

"I believe you, Mike. This is going to really piss off Libby Frank, though."

"My guess is that she's the reason Edith didn't come forward before now," Mike offered.

"I still haven't heard any objections from you, Lance," the judge said.

"I have none."

"Smart man," she replied.

The bailiff knocked on the door escorted Edith into the room. The judge smiled at her pastel hair; Edith was favoring the green end of the spectrum today.

"So Edith, you want to testify?"

"Yes, Your Honor. You have the wrong man on trial—"

Before she could say anymore, Judge Service silenced her. "That's what the trial is all about, and I'll hear what you have to say in the courtroom, not back here. My next question has already been answered. It seems that you do have relevant information as to the guilt or innocence of the accused, so I will allow you to testify as a surprise witness.

"However, I also must advise you that the District Attorney has the right to cross examine you, and that if you testify, you will most likely no longer be anonymous. Even if I order that your identity be kept private, which I will, this trial has been so public that such a ruling would be ludicrous. Right now, you have anonymity for two reasons: because of your age when the crime occurred, and because of the nature of the crime. That will essentially be lost as soon as you take the stand. Do you understand?"

"Yes. I do," Edith replied with great confidence.

The judge smiled. *She does take after her mother.*

# Chapter 35

Mary Sykes was an experienced and thorough researcher. However, as much as she tried, she could find no record of the personal property of Marc Legrande, tutor to the staff of Thomas Jefferson when he was in Paris. Other than some vague references in Jefferson's diary to a few boxes of papers that he could not bring with him on his way back to the U.S., there was nothing linking Legrande to Jefferson—and there was no trace of the papers.

She looked away from the laptop screen, exhausted and disappointed, logging off from the university database. She made herself a cup of tea and looked at the clock. In a few hours, she would have to meet with her class, and she had not yet been to bed. Looking at the photo of her father and mother she had on the shelf laden with books sitting above the television, she said, "Sorry, Dad. I thought I could help, but it looks like I screwed up."

She took out her phone to call the airline and cancel her flight to Paris, since it would be a waste of time. The archives had informed her that there were no papers in their collection from Marc Legrande. She checked with the archives in London and there in Amsterdam with the same result. He went to London and then died soon after. Other than the death notice in the London archives, everything else was a dead end. She shook her head. Such a sad end for a smart young man, and all because the world went crazy and he happened to be related to a Marquis. A distant cousin, she recalled as she dialed the phone number for the airlines, hoping they'd refund her money, but suspecting she'd probably have to take it as a credit.

Before she completed her call, her phone rang. It was Paul. She checked the time, and realized it was late in Virginia, so he probably had something.

"Hi, Paul."

"Hi, Mary, sorry to call this late."

"What's up?"

"You hit a dead end with Legrande, I see."

"Yeah." She'd sent him an email earlier.

"I had a thought, though."

"Shoot."

"Did you try his royal relative? The Marquis De Compte?"

"Wasn't he killed in the Reign of Terror?"

"Actually, no, he managed to talk his way out of being executed because he had a reputation of being fair to the people who worked for him. He was a local judge and people took their cases to him from miles away because he had a reputation for impartiality. A lot of people spoke up on his behalf, so he was allowed to go into exile instead of facing the guillotine. Guess where he went?"

"Amsterdam?"

"Close. Utrecht. It was a more important city back then than Amsterdam, and much more welcoming for Catholics. Maybe he took possession of his cousin's papers? The man was about sixty when he left, but he never returned to France. The Marquis lived into his early seventies, and his cousin was his only relative. The line died with him."

"That's beyond a long shot. You might as well buy a lottery ticket and pray you hit it, but I can log into their archives through the university server. Utrecht has a reputation for having one of the best city archives in Europe."

They chatted a little more and said goodbye.

She ran the Marquis's name through the archives search engine, and then she booked a train ticket online to Utrecht for Monday. She went to bed to get a few hours of sleep before her class. After class she'd have the weekend to rest up. Mary was a realist and didn't allow herself to indulge in false hope, but she did grant herself one tiny flicker of optimism.

# Chapter 36

The courtroom went silent as Edith Frank was called to the stand. She was sworn in and sat in the witness box, looking intently at Mike.

"Edith, please tell the court your relationship to this case."

"I am the victim, the person who was molested."

"Then you must be the one who brought the charges against my client."

"No."

"No?"

"No. Professor Sykes never touched me. Ever," she said. "Except when I threw up and passed out in his class," she added quickly. There was some laughter.

"When did that happen?"

"The first day of school."

"Were you ill?"

"I had an abortion that morning." She paused, and quietly added, "I was supposed to go home and rest, but I didn't."

"I'm sorry to hear that. It must have been traumatic," Mike said gently, "but I need to ask you—and this is the crux of the prosecution's case—was Gil Sykes the father?"

"No."

"Did you ever have any intimate relations with the defendant, Gil Sykes?"

"No."

"Did Gil Sykes ever indicate that he wanted to have relations with you?

"No."

"Thank you, Edith. I have no further questions, Your Honor."

"Would you like to cross, Mr. Hendricks?"

"Yes, Your Honor." Lance came over to the witness box and looked at Edith for a few seconds. "Edith, is it true that you signed up to take another class with the defendant this spring, and it was in that class that you passed out?"

"Yes."

"Did he force you to take the class with him?"

"Did he what?" Edith was dumbfounded.

"Did he make you take the class with him?"

"Why on earth would he do that?" Edith said.

"To keep you close to him."

"That's ridiculous!"

"Then the answer is no?"

"The answer is no. He never even asked me to take another class, let alone tried to make me."

"Isn't it true that you ran out of his office last December in tears?"

"Yes, but—"

"Yes?"

"Yes. I was upset. I'd just found out I was pregnant."

"And you were upset because Gil Sykes wouldn't admit that it was his baby?"

"No. That's the dumbest idea in the world."

"Is it? You like professor Sykes?"

"Yes. He's a good teacher."

"That's all?"

"Yes."

"You don't have a crush on him at all? You wouldn't lie for him?"

"No." She was losing patience.

"He is not the father of the child you aborted?"

"No."

"Are you sure?"

"Mr. Hendricks," Edith changed her tone completely, defusing any anger she had, and spoke to him like he was a child, "you've known me most of my life. You've been to my house on many occasions for dinner with my mom and dad, and for political fundraisers and socials. And you know that I have an IQ north of 140? You know that's why I'm in college even though I've just turned sixteen, right?"

"Yes," he said.

"So you'd think I'd be smart enough to know who it was that I had sex with?" She smiled sweetly, and the audience erupted in laughter.

The judge beat her gavel for order.

"So if not Gil Sykes, who was it who you slept with? You didn't get pregnant on your own, did you?" Lance asked, recovering command of the room.

"I'd rather not say," Edith replied.

Judge Service said, "Edith, you have to say. That's what court is all about. If Gil Sykes is innocent as you claim, then who's guilty?"

"I don't want to get him in trouble."

"He already got himself in trouble," the judge said.

"Peter," Edith said after a long pause.

"Peter?" Lance asked.

"Yes. Peter Morton, Professor Sykes's teaching assistant. We were at a party, and things just happened. We got carried away. It wasn't his fault.

I was willing. It was a mistake. There was no molesting."

"How many men have you had these sorts of mistakes with?" Lance asked, changing direction. "How often do you get *carried away*, as you put it?"

"What?"

"How many men have you had sex with?" Lance asked, breaking the very important rule about asking a question he didn't have the answer to, but trying to attack a woman's reputation in a sexual harassment trial, or any case where sex is involved, while usually a strategy for the defense, was a commonplace tactic.

"Just Peter."

"And how often did you have sex with Peter?" Lance asked, breaking the rule again. He hadn't gotten the answer he'd hoped for.

"Just once," she said quietly. "It was my first time." Her voice grew stronger as she said, "Like I said, it just happened. And it was a mistake. Not the sex, but not using birth control. That was the stupidest thing I ever did. I should have known better."

Lance looked at the jury. He knew from their faces they understood and believed every word she said. She had their sympathy, something no prosecutor wants to see in a jury. In fact, a few of them were giving *him* hostile looks.

"No further questions."

After a long pause, Mike Miller stood. "Your Honor, I move for dismissal of the case in light of this witness's testimony."

Judge Service took her time, and then gave Gary Sime and Dr. Bill both a very long, hard look. "Sexual harassment, especially sexual harassment where a person in a position of trust solicits sex from someone who has no power, is a disgusting crime, and one that has been tolerated by society for far too long. There is a world of difference between sexual harassment and thoughtless, or even stupid, sexual behavior, although I cannot excuse the circumstances in this case, and Peter Morton will be duly charged.

"However, to use this crime as a political tool, to have someone accused so that you can defer blame from your organization because of a history of tolerance of this sort of crime is unconscionable."

She looked directly at Gary, who looked genuinely terrified. "And to knowingly falsely accuse someone of this crime not only trivializes it but shows such a profound dearth of moral character that it gives me pause, especially in the case of people who are supposed to be in charge of the education of the young.

"This trial should have never happened. It was a waste of the court's time and a trivialization of a serious crime that has a shattering life-changing impact on the victim."

She turned to Mike. "I have to agree with you, Counselor." She rapped her gavel. "The case against Gilbert Sykes for the charge of sexual harassment is dismissed."

There was so much noise and confusion that no one heard the bailiff say, "All rise," nor did anyone notice when the judge left the courtroom. Justice Service didn't mind. Even though she was still angry that the charges had even been brought, she knew she'd just dodged the potentially worst political bullet of her career.

Edith went over to Gil, "I'm so sorry, Professor Sykes. I thought no one would even charge you since it was so stupid. Then I couldn't believe it went this far. I just found out today about the letter … and who wrote it."

"I know," Gil said. "It was Peter."

"Right. But … how?"

"Deduction. It was pretty obvious. Who else could it have been? But I'm sure it wasn't his idea."

"What'll happen to him?"

"I have no idea, but he's in a lot of trouble. You know a good criminal lawyer, Mike?"

Mike smiled and handed Edith his card. "Give this to Peter if you see him."

"I will see him. If only to tell him what an asshole he is," Edith said.

She left, and Gil and Mike went out for a late breakfast. Gil had been living on coffee for the past two days; now, suddenly, he was terrifically hungry. He also needed one more piece of legal advice from Mike Miller.

# Chapter 37

Sasha Korbet was on the phone when Phil, the editor-in-chief of the *Hudson Valley Journal,* motioned for her to come to his office. She was trying to contact her leads from the courthouse, but no one was returning any of her calls. She went into the cramped office where he spent most of his time in front of his 30-inch computer monitor putting the finishing touches on the daily paper that was now his sole responsibility. Since they'd been bought out by MaxiNews, two jobs had been made into one, and half the staff had been either fired or forced to take part-time positions.

"Have a seat." He pointed to the only chair that wasn't covered with boxes or papers. "How's it going, Sasha?"

"Okay, Phil," she said with her eyebrow raised.

"I was wondering if you could tell me a little about that story you ran on the professor who was accused of sexual harassment, Gilbert Sykes?"

"I wrote several stories about him."

"In particular the one we ran in bold on the front page about Bradbury College covering up old charges of sexual harassment by Professor Sykes."

"I got the tip from a reliable source."

"Who?"

"You know I can't say. It's anonymous, but it's from a guy who is very well placed to know."

"Maybe. That all depends on if the information happens to be true, now, doesn't it?" Phil looked at her, and he was starting to shake. "I ran all of the scandal you dug up on that man and the school because I trusted you, and you know how our mutual employer likes nothing better than a juicy scandal about colleges, and in particular liberal college professors. But this might just blow up in our faces, Sasha."

"Why?"

"The professor has filed a libel and defamation suit against the paper and the company that owns us naming you as the prime source of libel," he announced. "Because of the trial that you helped precipitate, the DA's office actually *really* did a thorough and impartial investigation that is now part of the public record, and that investigation totally exonerates him. They found nothing at all, nada, zilch, nothing." He stopped to mop his brow with a tissue before continuing. "So, Sasha, please tell me you vetted this story? Did you ask the usual questions? Do some digging?

Look up at least one old student or colleague?"

The look on her face answered his question.

"But they could have covered it up so well that no one can find the information," she said quickly.

"That's your defense? It could have happened, but no one can find out anything about it? That's how they prove aliens came to the earth to abduct little babies, for Christ's sake! *You can't prove it didn't happen*! Please don't tell me you didn't try to at least corroborate your information from another source? Just one other person who would be in a position to know for sure? Did you check to see if your source had an agenda? Or maybe that this could be just an opinion, or just some rumor making its way through the community?

"Right now, we could even get sued by Bradbury College because you outright said they covered up information about repeated felonies—although I'm sure they'd have good reasons not to, since they actually did cover up other felonies, just not this time. Professor Sykes, on the other hand, has nothing to lose and everything to gain."

"Well, my source had given me plenty of information in the past that turned out to be true, especially on the coach and the cover up."

"Yes, but you must have investigated those, too?"

"Sure I did."

"Tell me you just didn't take your source's word for this one?"

Sasha opened her mouth, closed it, and went to her desk. She packed up her things in a cardboard copy-paper box and left without a word.

The process server caught up with her later that afternoon at her apartment.

# Chapter 38

Gary sauntered into the conference room. Dr. Bill was there with Libby Frank and Gil Sykes. Gary had been waiting for this meeting, but now that it was here, he wasn't as confident he'd be able to talk his way out of the mess he knew he was in.

"Gil, glad to see you," he said cheerily, extending his hand.

"Hello, Gary," Gil said, ignoring Gary's hand. "I'm sure you are."

"I was pulling for you. You must be happy that mess is all cleared up?"

"Actually, I'd have rather not gone through it in the first place, but what's done is done," Gil said. *Especially since you caused most of it,* he added in his head.

"You know Libby Frank?" Dr. Bill said. "She's the new chair of the board of trustees."

"Congratulations, Libby," Gary said a little too brightly.

"Thank you, Gary." Her smile didn't reach her eyes.

"Gary, it has come to our attention that you've been in communication with a member of the press, Sasha Korbet, I think her name is," Dr. Bill said. *Now tell me you don't really know her, you asshole.*

Gary responded as if on cue.

"Not sure if I really know her, Bill," Gary said shaking his head.

"Hmm," Dr. Bill replied while fiddling with his phone. He found the picture that Christina had sent him of Gary's cell phone with an incoming call from Sasha Korbet. "I was wondering how her number would be on your cell phone. That is your phone, correct? I always thought that custom-made case was a little tacky."

Gary looked at the photo and turned pale, and then he decided to go on the attack.

"If that's my phone, then someone invaded my privacy. I want to know who it was."

Gil and Libby burst out laughing; Dr. Bill only smiled.

"Where did you get the information about Gil Sykes having a history with some of his students?" Dr. Bill asked, changing the subject.

"Well, from …."

"From me? Were you going to say?" Dr. Bill said. "Did you bother checking it out? Didn't I say it was only a rumor, Gary? Didn't I say to keep quiet about it?"

Gary's mouth fell open.

"It happened to be a rumor that I started myself in order to trap you. Sorry, Gil."

"Couldn't think of anything else, Bill?" Gil replied.

"That's not fair," Gary exclaimed.

"You know what's not fair? Being a miserable cheat who'll do or say anything to get promoted. Do you really want my job so badly that you'd try to destroy someone else? Put him in jail? What the hell is wrong with you?

"Libby Frank is here in her capacity as representative of the trustees, and she and I are both ready to accept your resignation. If you feel that you're not being treated fairly, then you are more than welcome to complain to HR, the trustees, or even file a lawsuit. In fact, please be my guest, and then we can make everything you did public. Not to mention some of your, shall we say, unusual expense reports?"

Gary flinched.

"You think we're so stupid that we don't know how much a weekend in a hotel in Las Vegas should cost? We are more than ready to dismiss you for cause, so I suggest you write your resignation. I want it on my desk in an hour and you off campus by the end of the day. The choice is yours, Gary."

***

Millie Cavanaugh burst into the office of the Dean of the School of Business with the dean's secretary trailing behind. The secretary looked angry but threw up her hands. She would have had to physically stop Millie in order to keep her from bursting into the room. The dean motioned for the secretary to go. Millie stood in the middle of the room, quaking with anger.

"Can I help you, Professor Cavanaugh?"

"What is this nonsense?" Millie said, holding a piece of paper out, her hand shaking with rage.

The dean took it and quickly read it. "That's your schedule for next semester," he explained.

"I know what it is, dammit. Why am I only teaching sections of Intro to Business at eight o'clock in the morning?"

"We decided that it might be best for senior faculty to reach out to our freshman and teach some of the intro courses, you know, to help with student retention.

"Bullshit."

"Excuse me?"

"You heard me."

"Millie, I think you don't understand. This was the best deal I could get for you." He waited for a few moments for his words to sink in. "As far as the president and trustees are concerned, you should be fired."

On what grounds?"

"On moral grounds. For having sexual relations with a graduate student? Peter Morton, I think his name is? Not to mention the trustees take a dim view of letters that cause as much trouble as yours did."

"So he gets off scot-free? He's the one who wrote the damn letter."

"No. He's facing serious charges and could go to jail for having sex with a minor, but Libby Frank is actually defending him." There was another long silence. The dean changed tone. "You're smart, Millie, but the rest of us are smart, too. And you aren't always the smartest person in the room. There is a world of difference between a young graduate student making a stupid mistake and someone who deliberately decides to lie to get a colleague in trouble. You should know that difference. I suggest you start going to bed earlier so you'll be bright and fresh for your classes. It might cut into your social life, but who knows? It could improve your teaching. And next time you want to speak with me, please make an appointment."

# Chapter 39

Mary Sykes blew the dust from her nose into a tissue. It had been a short train ride to Utrecht. She'd discovered that the Marquis de Compte had been a complete slob when it came to record keeping. His papers were a jumble of personal letters, court decisions, and bills from the day-to-day running of his estates. It looked as if he'd thrown everything into crates in a hurry, and never bothered opening them again when he got to Utrecht. The truth was, as Mary saw it, that he probably expected to return to his estates in France in the near future, but all of his land had been confiscated by the Republic, and the Marquis died in exile.

She was covered in dust, and wiped the sweat from her forehead, leaving a trail of white tissue behind. Her hope was evaporating.

Her phone rang. It was her brother Jason, who hadn't called her in weeks.

"Hi, Jason."

Hi, Sis. Sorry I haven't called. School suddenly got a lot harder."

"Yes, that's called sophomore year. You can't wing it any longer no matter how smart you are. Just read the books, little brother, and it'll get a lot easier."

"You tried to tell me, big sister. Mea culpa. How are you anyway?"

She almost burst into tears. She quickly told him about the hours of research and digging through dusty boxes crammed with papers and letters, and all the help she had from Paul in her fruitless quest to find the pirate Charter and connect it unequivocally to Thomas Jefferson. She related to him how frustrating it had been trying to chase down Thomas Jefferson's papers and how every time she thought she had a good lead, she'd hit a dead end, and had just hit another with her futile search of the Marquis' personal papers.

Jason was sympathetic, but then asked a quick question. "You said the papers belonged to his cousin, right?"

"Yes, Marc Legrande."

"Wouldn't his uncle have stored the papers under his cousin's name in order to keep them separate from his own personal papers, especially if he planned on returning to France and to his property after the Revolution was over?"

There was a long pause, and Jason thought maybe they had been disconnected when his sister said, "If you were here, I would hug you until you turned blue and kiss you on the mouth!"

"That would be weird, and just a little disgusting," Jason said.

"I love you, brother."

"Thanks, but don't go off the deep end. It was only an idea. It might not work. It could be another dead end. One question, though."

"What?"

"Who's Paul?"

# Chapter 40

*A year later*

Gil was looking out of his window gazing at the polar white Mercedes that was worth about a year of his salary sitting in his driveway. Marion came up to him and put her arms around his waist.

"Nice car," she said.

"Yes, it is."

"Perhaps a little ostentatious?"

"No, not at all. It's insanely, outrageously ostentatious, but I've needed a new car for a long time now."

"Yes, and wasn't it wonderful of MaxiNews to buy you such a nice one?"

"Should I send them a thank you note along with a photo?"

"Don't bother. But I've got to tell you, Mary thinks it makes us look like we're a family of gangsters."

"It does look out of place in this neighborhood, but tell her gangsters are all obligated to drive black cars. There's some sort of agreement or contract they all have to sign, I think. And Jason keeps bugging me to drive it. What part of the word *never* does he not understand?"

"Be nice to him. He's the one who helped Mary find that paper, that Charter, that proved you and Valerie were right."

"Yeah. That was great. Just to see all of those critics finally shut up, even that ass Lenny Trout. At least for now," Gil said. "I'm sure someone will challenge whether or not it really belonged to Jefferson since it was found in another person's private papers, but I can wait for that shoe to drop. Academics can be exceptionally good at ignoring the obvious."

Gil had looked at the sales figures for the book that morning. He had insisted that Valerie get seventy-five percent of the royalties. She'd wanted to split them evenly, but he prevailed by arguing that the whole project had been her idea. Even his twenty-five percent was proving to be a worthwhile amount of money. Along with the undisclosed settlement he got from MaxiNews to settle his libel suit, money was suddenly not at all a concern.

He'd spoken to Valerie that morning; she was settling in at her new job at Duke University. Gil had to admit he was a little jealous that she'd gotten such an excellent offer, but he also could probably get another job if he wanted just on the strength of the book and get a better deal from a better school. An academic bestseller, he knew, opened a lot of doors.

Gil was sitting in the living room, wondering idly if he should make a large donation to Planned Parenthood in the name of the CEO of MaxiNews. Marion came back from the kitchen with a cup of coffee.

"I'm thinking of taking a year off," he said. "Bradbury will give me an unpaid year's leave."

"Wow. How generous of them."

"Well, that's how they operate. Nothing's going to change that. I thought we might do some traveling."

"Sounds fine." Marion was smiling.

"You knew already?"

"Of course. You always leave the browser on the last place you visited on the internet. I couldn't possibly avoid noticing that you were looking at plane tickets and destinations. Unless you are fleeing the Russian mob, I figured we were going to be traveling soon."

"Well, there's the thing with the Russian mob, too, but I can handle them. After last year, I can handle anything," Gil said.

"I'm up for some travel, but who will man the ramparts? Who will hold back the barbarians at the gates? The next Dark Age?"

"Someone else?"

At that moment, Mary came through the front door. She was visiting for a few weeks before going back to Amsterdam to start graduate work and had just driven back from Virginia where she had spent a week visiting Paul. His girlfriend wasn't at all happy with her being there, and Mary got the distinct impression that Paul's relationship with his girlfriend was not altogether that solid. Mary was holding her suitcase at a funny angle. One of the wheels had come off on her last trip home, so she had to tilt it to one side in order to maneuver it. She came in and sat on the couch. The suitcase immediately flopped over dead on the ground, looking like a small, dirty, red coffin.

"That was a long drive. It would have been much nicer in your new car, Dad."

"I'm sure it would have," Gil said.

"You need new luggage, Mary," Marion said.

"Please don't buy me anything."

"Oh, I'm not going to buy you anything, but your father will. Right, Gil?"

"Why not? It's time, Mary. That bag looks like it's about ready to fall apart," Gil said.

"I know. I just like it," she said. "It makes me look well-travelled."

"It makes you look indigent."

"Dad!"

"You need to let go, Mary. You need some new luggage, if only so when you fly back to Amsterdam your clothes will make it there with you, and not end up in the bottom of the luggage compartment of the plane."

"I don't know. I really want to buy my things myself. You two have done enough for me. I'm too old to have my Mommy and Daddy buying me stuff."

"Don't let your brother know, but I'll let you drive my new car to the mall—but *only* if you promise me that I can buy you a new set of luggage when we get there."

"You've got a deal!" Mary smiled as she got off the couch holding her hand out for the ignition key fob. "Let's go!"

"And while we're gone," Gil said to his wife, "why don't you figure out our first destination?"

# Epilogue

The TV was on, and the latest scandal was being reported as breaking news. One of Patrick Henri's interns had secretly made a video of him begging to have sex with her; she had obviously refused. He could be clearly seen in his tighty whitey, which accentuated his chemically induced erection, while screaming hysterically that he would make sure she failed her internship, ruin her chances to graduate college, and ruin any career she might have in TV. The video was so popular it had crashed the social media servers. His show had instantly disappeared from the lineup and had been replaced with reruns of a police procedural that had been off the air for several years.

# About the Author

 Joe Zeppetello is an educator who teaches writing and writing theory. He has published a novel, *Daring to Eat a Peach*, various short stories, nonfiction, and has a keen interest in photography. *These Truths* is his second published novel.

Joe has worn many hats over the years. He's worked in a silver mill in Colorado and been a professional cook, waiter, and bartender in several different venues, including downtown Chicago. In the early 1980s, he ran a health food luncheonette, and was a substitute teacher for the local high school. For ten years, he worked as an adjunct lecturer at several colleges in the Hudson Valley. He finished his doctoral degree in 1996 and worked for about twenty years as a faculty administrator in charge of the writing program and writing center at Marist College, where he currently teaches English.

*These Truths* is the result of Joe's speculation about the consequences of finding a truth that would be unpopular to the majority of Americans about a Founding Father and cast doubt about the origins of our Declaration of Independence and the Constitution. What would happen to the people who discovered it? How would the issue play out in social media and the press?

Joe lives in the Catskill Mountains with his wife and is presently working on another novel.

Like and follow *These Truths* on Facebook, and learn more about Joe at http://www.joezeppetello.com/

**ALL THINGS THAT MATTER PRESS**


FOR MORE INFORMATION ON TITLES AVAILABLE FROM
ALL THINGS THAT MATTER PRESS, GO TO
http://allthingsthatmatterpress.com
or contact us at
allthingsthatmatterpress@gmail.com

www.ingramcontent.com/pod-product-compliance
Lightning Source LLC
Chambersburg PA
CBHW070513260626
47161CB00004B/1539